OUR SOUL –
A TRANSWORLDLY
ENERGY COMPLEX
The Soul Pervades All Aspects of Our Lives

Hermann de Witt

Translated by Johanna Ellsworth, MA

OUR SOUL – A TRANSWORLDLY ENERGY COMPLEX
The Soul Pervades All Aspects of Our Lives
Copyright © Hermann de Witt 2002

All Rights Reserved

No part of this book may be reproduced in any form
by photocopying or by any electronic or mechanical means,
including information storage or retrieval systems,
without permission in writing from both the copyright
owner and the publisher of this book.

ISBN 978-3-7322-7360-7

Manufactured and published by
BoD - Books on Demand, Norderstedt,
Germany

MIX
Papier aus verantwortungsvollen Quellen
Paper from responsible sources
FSC® C105338

OUR SOUL – A TRANSWORLDLY ENERGY COMPLEX
The Soul Pervades All Aspects of Our Lives

Contents

Introduction		ix
I	Fundamental Principles	13
	The Soul = Function of the Body?	13
	The Traditional Trinity: Body–Soul–Mind	14
	Intermediate Links as Mediators	15
	Life Energy (Vitality) and Drive (Tendency)	16
	The Discovery of the Individual Energy of our Soul	17
II	General Analogies Between Body and Soul	19
	Three Basic Tendencies of the Soul *analogous to* the Body	19
	Three Main Qualities of the Soul *analogous to* Main Parts of the Body	21
	Four Life Circles of the Human Soul *analogous to* the Body	23
III	The Soul of All Creatures as a Formation of Tendencies	25
	The Universal Character of Tendencies	25
	Stability of Tendencies *analogous to* Inertia of Matter	26
	Hierarchy of Tendencies *analogous to* the Hierarchy of a People	32
	Individual Tendency Formation *analogous to* the Texture of a Rope	38

	Humanity *analogous to* Fabric	41
IV	**Human Tendency Groups *analogous to* Worldly Forms of Energy**	46
	Person and Personality	46
	Psychic Drives of the Personality *analogous to* Worldly Forms of Energy	48
	Mental Drives of Personality *analogous to* Radiation Energy	55
	Four Levels of Tendencies *analogous to* Additional Forms of Energy	64
V	**Embodiment and Re-Embodiment**	71
	Embodiment of our Soul *analogous to* the Building of a House	71
	Circulation of our Soul *analogous to* Year and Day	78
VI	**Immortality of our Soul as a Tendency Formation**	86
	The Law of Mass and Energy Conservation	86
	Expansion Through Atomic Energy	87
	Unlimited Ethereal Energy	90
	Sphere of Influence of the Soul	92
	The Rule of Tendency Changes	93
	Immortality of the Individual Soul	96
VII	**Meditation as Mystical Solution for our Soul**	99
	Introduction	99
	Mental Preconditions for Meditation	101
	Conditions of Main Consciousness	102

VIII Summary 105
- The Soul as an Energy Complex 105
- The Soul as a Formation of Tendencies 106
- The Embodiment of our Soul 107
- The Re-Embodiment of our Soul 107
- The Immortality of our Soul 108

Epilogue 111

Bibliography 113

INTRODUCTION

Haven't certain similarities between the eye and a camera, the ear and a microphone been emphasised again and again to give examples of how the sensors of a robot function *analogous to* a living organism? When comparing the two, however, it should not be overlooked that sensors are merely *passive* measuring instruments, while our organs of sense are backed by concerns of our *psyche* that enable the close collaboration between the body and the soul. Let the author illustrate this:

> Your ear *longs* for the voice of your beloved mate.
> Your nose *prefers* certain flower scents and most likely detests 'country air' after the farmer has sprayed dung on his fields.
> Your tongue *tastes* different types of food before it is being offered and *selects* accordingly.

It is *not* the physical organ itself – which is almost identical in most humans – which does the selecting, but rather the *mental energy* that stands behind it, be it urge and impulse, longing and desire, wish and need, craving or, as the author calls it in general, a certain individual *tendency* that is usually accompanied by its opposite.

On the other hand, it does *not* matter at all to a camera, microphone and other *sensors* what they *register*. They work neutrally (objectively), while all of our senses are biased (subjective) by the mental tendencies that occupy the senses. Out of a rich selection of registered pictures, sounds, smells, tastes and structures, only that which is (consciously) registered *corresponds* with particular *tendencies*. By the way, this tendentious character of registration results in a *subconscious* distortion of our 'image of the world'.

Of course, each sensor has a particular area of reception and can only transmit a certain section of reality. However, that is not the case for the *function* of the senses: for instance, while the

ix

frequency range of the human eye contains only one octave between red and violet, the soul, in *addition*, has complicated 'filters' built into each organ of sense according to its tendencies.

You may want a few words on how this thesis came into being. During his daily meditation, which the author has been practising for forty-five years, he has experienced the soul as an *energy complex*, and anyone else who meditates will have a very similar experience on his or her way to inner freedom. In order to differentiate between these *mental* energies and the *worldly* energies known to him as a physicist, the author has called them *transworldly* energies. They are obviously a lot more refined than all physical energies and therefore remain invisible to the eye of the modern human being.

That is even more astonishing when you realise that today's uneasy questions: 'Where are we from? Where are we going to?' (15) could not surface for many millenniums. In the past, people were still tied to the *parapsychological* relations of the soul between this world and the other world; they still experienced the presence of disembodied souls and saw the souls on their return to the mother's womb.

As a non-religious counter-movement to today's materialism, *research into dying* is gaining more and more fans, a great part of which is due to the courageous and much honoured *E Kübler-Ross* (17). She demonstrates to the contemporary sceptic that, after leaving its worldly prison, his or her soul takes its whole personality into the 'country beyond'.

The meditation mentioned above disclosed areas of consciousness to the author that were *beyond* all processes of thinking, whereby he found many *allegories* from daily life. His first book, *ANALOGIK*, ie: *ANALOGICS* was born out of his hobby. *Analogies* are simply similes and allegories necessary to wise men and founders of religion when they want to tell other human beings of heavenly energies, laws and higher beings. The imagery of poets is especially rich with allegories.

The following chapter will familiarise you with the *basics* of analogics. Section I offers you arguments *against* a *materialistic* world view. You will learn the method of analogics depending on your personality structure of body–soul–mind in Section II. This traditional trinity is supplemented by intermediate links between the body and soul in Section III, and you will discover the difference between life energy (vitality) and driving force (tendency), with the aid of analogies on your driving style, in Section IV.

The five-page summary at the end of the text is recommended for a quick overview.

Chapter I
FUNDAMENTAL PRINCIPLES

The Soul = Function of the Body?

The machine theory for living creatures found its most extreme expression in *L'homme machine,* i.e., the human being as a machine (1748 by *Lamettrie*). This *materialistic* model was later supported by the science of biochemistry and the triumphant success of electronic calculators, also called electronic brains by the public. The *unwarrantableness* of that theory was proven after World War II by noted scientists. A few indications should suffice here.

Since all healthy bodies respond to the same biochemical rules, they should react very much alike to drugs such as *alcohol.* While taking into consideration that a person can get used to alcohol, there is still a wide range of *individual* behaviour: some individuals become tired, while others begin to philosophise; some feel the need to be loved and others again turn aggressive.

How does this variety of behaviour correspond with the claim made by a professor that 'the *soul* is a *function* of the *brain*', which he still wants to sell to his students?

What can *dream* experiences teach us about the relationship between the soul and the body? In our dreams, we can experience any kind of activity, even flying (floating without the aid of an aeroplane), while our body lies in bed without moving. Apart from dreams caused by physical conditions – such as noise, cold or heat, digestion problems, etc. – there are other types of dreams that give evidence of the *independence* of body and soul: *erotic* dreams, on the one hand, can occur without any physical symptoms, while on the other hand an erection of the penis can occur due to physical influences without any dream images.

Do you belong to those who claim that they never dream? They do dream like everyone else, but they cannot *remember* their dreams after waking up. Even though this ability to remember is restricted for most humans, it can be improved through practice. *Meaningful* dreams usually *stay* in one's memory for many years. Even most *animals* dream, and humans who are stopped from dreaming by repetitive interruptions of their sleep become ill. *Day*dreaming, which is also widespread, is similar to night dreams insofar as the *functions* of the senses – but not the *organs* of the senses – are temporarily eliminated and the consciousness is filled with memories, desires and fantasies. Our dreams, therefore, prove a certain *separation* between body and soul.

The Traditional Trinity: Body–Soul–Mind

Even though these three factors are emotionally familiar to us, it is probably difficult to put their mutual relationships into words. Here analogies can assist us; they are very useful when treating qualities such as soul and mind. In the following *analogy table*, we set the traditional human trinity opposite two corresponding qualities, structures or objects with just as many *subgroups*. If we place these subgroups suitably into the three lines, we also get close relationships within one line in accordance with the 'second analogy law of corresponding parts' (7). Such analogy tables were widespread in the Middle Ages, when people were still more interested in qualities than in quantities. The three terms – analogy, simile and allegory – mean almost the same.

Person		Science	Causality
mind		information	cause
soul	*analogous to*	energy	conditions
body		matter, mass	effect

Figure 1

In this analogy formula Figure 1, we limit the human being to an ego-conscious *person*, excluding toddlers as long as they still speak of themselves in the third person.

In the second column, we find the pillars of natural sciences: information, energy and matter (mass). Of these subgroups, energy on the centre line has a close relationship with the soul:

| soul | *analogous to* | energy |

Figure 2

which is the central theme of this book: *Our Soul – A Transworldly Energy Complex*. Section 2 of Chapter IV is dedicated to analogies for psychic drives of the personality, while the no less important mental drives are treated in Section 3.

Why have three links been listed under causality in Figure 1, instead of the usual two, i.e., cause and effect? The absolute necessity of *conditions* as the third link to causality can immediately be understood when we take *electrical energy* as an example: depending on the electric appliance you plug in, you receive as a result light, heat, power, sound and/or picture. Therefore, the appliances offer the various conditions for the *transformation* of the very same electrical energy. Thus, the subgroups on the centre line – soul, energy, conditions – carry out a *mediating function* between the links of the upper and lower lines.

Intermediate Links as Mediators

It is an old issue of dispute whether the *soul* is made of any *matter* or not. Whenever the existence of delicate matter was attributed to the soul, it was identified with one of its higher and more refined bodies that are freed upon terrestrial death. We find this attitude among the ancient Egyptians and in many other cultures. However, when the soul is considered the highest principle of all, it remains completely independent even from the most refined embodiment. This attitude is widespread among the old Indian philosophers, whose highest principle (*atma*) can be translated as mind as well as with soul.

Similar approaches surfaced later among Christian thinkers; they, however, emphasised the *dualism* between the '*eternal soul*' and the '*sinful body*' too much, which made extreme developments in church and science possible. In that aspect, the *Indian philosophers* were better off, since neither their monistic nor their dualistic schools succumbed to the temptation to the extent that Western schools did to claim *either* the soul – mind as the highest principle *or* the earthly body as the last reality (within materialism). That difference between the East and the West has

15

to do with the fact that the East remained more conscious of the delicate *intermediate links*. But where the experiences of a psychic-mental reality diminish, speculations and dogmatism can spread unrestricted.

We can put this wilderness of speculation aside, since we have an *experienced* scientific definition of *energy* at our disposal that takes possession of our civilisation more and more. For our subject – the soul as a transworldly energy complex – we only need to *transfer* the definition of energy as a rough matter to psychic-mental areas, as the author has done by his definition:

Tendencies = psychic-mental energies that determine the kind, direction and extent of all life processes

Figure 3

We have to go beyond the traditional division of the human being into three aspects by not only taking the *rough*-mattered *terrestrial* body, but also the *fine*-mattered *ethereal* body into consideration. It has become known under different names: od-body or fluidal body, energy body, etc. (which, however, you should not confuse with the astral body, which will be discussed later). Today, ethereal irradiation, particularly from the fingertips, can be made *visible* with the aid of the Kirlian photography method, while in the past one had to depend on statements made by clairvoyant individuals.

If your fingertips are sensitive enough, you can 'feel' the health aura of the *ethereal* body *above* the skin. Healing magnetism (22) is based on that, whereby a patient receives a massage of 'magnetic strokes' above the skin and is loaded with the healer's personal energy at the same time. An ethereal body that has been put back into harmony and strengthened will soon transfer its health to the terrestrial body controlled by it.

Life Energy (Vitality) and Drive (Tendency)

Since the *ethereal* body is often confused with the *astral* body, their different functions shall be explained here. The ethereal body is the carrier of life energy, while the more refined astral body is the carrier of our drive, which contains all our longings, desires and wishes, defined by the author as tendencies.

A strong *life energy* = vitality – as a karmic effect of a benevolent and permissive attitude – expresses itself in the health aura which radiates *joy of life*. On the other hand, persons with a weak life energy (especially sick and old people) have a tiring effect, because they unknowingly drain energy from other persons. Let us clarify the relationship between vitality and drive through an analogy:

| drive (tendency) | | driver (purposiveness) |
| life energy (vitality) | *analogous to* | car (engine power) |

Figure 4

A *passionate* individual is moved by a strong drive (a classical example is *Goethe*, whose extremely slanted handwriting expresses his strong inclination). When such a person has a strong vitality at the same time, they can perseveringly devote themselves to their passions, like a fast *driver* in a fast *car*. If, however, a passionate or otherwise very active person has only little vitality at his or her disposal, the said discrepancy will soon show itself as exhaustion or illness, equal to an ambitious driver who constantly overexerts the weak engine of his car.

In that case, the psychic disharmonies that *Goethe* also showed come out more obviously. On the other hand, you can still lead a healthy and successful life, if you have a harmonious personality, even if you have only little life energy at your disposal.

The Discovery of the Individual Energy of the Soul

Our Western civilisation, which has taken charge of the whole earth in the twentieth century, is the result of an extreme *extraversion*, or turning to the outside. To the same degree, attitude bore heavenly as well as devilish fruit in engineering, as the ability to come to grips with the *psychic-mental* inner world was *reduced*. It is practically non-existent with most people, a fact which, to a certain degree, confirms the claim of the materialists that 'soul = function of the body', insofar as the *conscious life* of the soul of our contemporaries is seriously limited.

At the same time, the function of thinking (intellect) has limited itself to the processing of sensory perceptions, whereby an *identification* with this thinking Ego emerges. The inner motives become *conscious* as desired objects and multifarious relationships with other persons. However, their soul life can only be disclosed *indirectly*. Even the Bible has already said that it is easier for us to discover the splinter in the eye of our neighbour than the beam in our own eye, which laments the general lack of self-criticism.

Is *self-criticism* proof of *self-knowledge* in its stricter meaning? Only if you have a distinct eagerness for a *deeper* self-knowledge, otherwise self-criticism – similar to a conflict of interests – tends to stay on the *surface of day consciousness*. In extreme situations, however, the armour of the *Ego* can *burst*, exposing deeper layers of being. Such extreme situations can be *triggered* by the loss of habitual orders (property, work, loved ones, health, home, etc.).

If you have been spared from similar fates, you may study the soul energy of other *characters* of *extreme expression*: successful individuals with ambition, *discoverers* with lust for adventure, inventors and *engineers* with tenacity, *revolutionaries* with fanaticism, *social reformers* with practical altruism, saints with conquest of worldly issues… The attentive observer will easily identify the *driving forces* of such outstanding personalities from the past and present, be they great benefactors or malefactors.

After you have sharpened your inner eye on some special cases, you are now able to turn to the 'anatomy' of the human soul. In Chapter II, we start with the skeleton of our soul. This will clarify more and more the close analogy between body and soul according to psychosomatics (27) – stemming from Greek *soma*, meaning body – which is slowly invading medicine. How could you relate to other persons if your soul did not express itself more or less through your body?

Chapter II
GENERAL ANALOGIES BETWEEN BODY AND SOUL

Three Basic Tendencies of the Soul *analogous to* the Body

Perhaps the *human being* really is the 'pearl of creation', even though he has biological disadvantages due to the fact that he walks on two legs. Even if we do not stem from the ape, our body shows a variety of *similarities* with the *animal kingdom*.

More than 2,500 years ago, *Buddha* saw only *degrees of difference*, which is why there are *transitions* between both realms during the course of incarnation. *Buddha* enforced these repeated claims with numerous examples and, on the other hand, pointed out *transitions between humans and gods*. The ways up and down are *open* to human beings when they change their soul, i.e., their tendency household accordingly. The fact that the Western world is distrustful of, or rejects outright, such Indian statements that are based on clairvoyant experiences is very understandable, due to its fixation on the day consciousness in space and time. But we have to cordially invite our pondering contemporaries to generalise the law of causality, which is familiar to them and has stood the test of the outer world, in the sense of the *karmic law*, and to extend the same to the *psychic-mental* areas. Then even the sceptical Western countries will be equally able to confirm the Indian claims.

The central issue of each soul is described by *Buddha* very generally as the *thirst of being*. This longing to *exist* on one of the many levels of being can only be satisfied if the soul is *embodied* or incarnated in the terrestrial world or a world of refined matter. The type of this embodiment naturally depends on the *qualities* of the soul and its karmic *merits and offences*. In our analogy Figure 5, we differentiate between three aspects of the thirst of being, which are opposite to three aspects of physical autonomy:

Thirst of Being of the Soul		Physical Autonomy of the Body
development self-assertion compensation	*analogous to*	growth self-preservation regeneration

Figure 5

The *development* of psychic functions *equals the growth* of the body, and occurs parallel to growth of the body during youth. However, the maturing process as psychic growth should continue into old age. The *power of growth* of *plants*, the explosive effect of tree roots, is particularly impressive. The same tendency is shown by humans during their 'plant-like period'. It can even happen that a growing child in a pregnant woman's womb can deprive the mother of essential nutritious substances for its own growth, if the woman takes in too little or unbalanced nutrition. That process can continue during the nursing period.

After birth, the newborn begins to breathe on its own, which is the beginning of the baby's own life. *Breathing* and *heartbeat* are two of the most obvious activities required by the *self-preservation* of the body. The act of breathing is right between controlled and uncontrolled functions. Even *Buddha* had to experience, prior to his awakening, that breathing – no matter how much he applied his willpower – can only be suppressed for a short time, and will then – even stronger than before – prove the drive for the preservation of life. The method of holding one's breath is, therefore, not suitable for suicide.

The self-preservation of the body is equal to the *self-assertion* of the soul, which expresses itself in nature when animals assert their usual territory. That drive occurs in many animals just as strongly as in humans, where we speak of the right to their house and home. Due to the said drive, even a *small animal* can successfully *defend* its habitat against *larger animals*, while it is forced to yield to the same rivals in open wilderness. Very similarly, *small nations* have successfully defended themselves at home against a multiple superior force of foreign armies and finally forced the aggressor to withdraw. *Material strategists*, however, apparently have not yet learned that *psychological lesson*.

We arrive at the bottom line of Figure 5. When a single part of the body is damaged or lost, there is the power to restore the former healthy condition, which is called *regeneration*. External and internal wounds heal by themselves, and damaged organs are restored. The replacement of limbs and organs, however, is limited to the lower animal species and most distinctive among plants. On the other side, the human body only has a low ability to regenerate itself, and it is rare that an arm cut off by a machine can be sewn back on to the body and is fully functional afterwards.

According to Figure 5, the regeneration of the body corresponds to the *compensation* of the *soul*, which must be distinguished from the body's ability to adjust. It is a known fact, for instance, that eunuchs compensate their inability to perform sexual love by loving sweets. A similar *shifting* in the *tendency structure* is found among *children deprived of parental love*. A grown man may be able to compensate disappointments with *workaholism*. In all these cases, the compensation takes place in the *soul*, since the replaced physical functions are *too* different for the body.

Three Main Qualities of the Soul *analogous to* Main Parts of the Body

So far, we have not yet taken the shape of the body into consideration. The following section is dedicated to the roughest division of animal and human, which is set out in the following analogy table:

Quality of the Soul		Main Parts of the Body
unrest (tendency of perception) action and reaction phlegm (habit)	*analogous to*	head limbs torso

Figure 6

Let us start with the bottom line. The *torso* contains the main section of the body, even though it is surpassed in length by the limbs. Fish seem to almost exclusively consist of torso, since they show barely any neckline. Fish also show us the principle of *phlegm* most clearly, since they can remain in one place for a long time without moving. They can achieve this without any effort due to the fact that they are carried by the water and are in static balance with their element.

The physical principle of *mass inertia* corresponds with habit, relaxation and phlegm (phlegmatic temper) on the *psychic* level. This does not only mean *rest* but also any kind of *habitual activity*. Any change to the usual rhythm is accompanied by strong resistance. Humans even deduce from any long tradition a habitual right, even if this is extremely barbaric.

Apart from the lowest species of animals, we find a number of *limbs* growing out of the torso. They can be shaped into fins, wings, legs or human arms. The limbs serve as a means of locomotion as well as a tool, a function which among birds is handled by the beak. The *psychic activity* corresponds to flexibility; the ability of the limbs to reach and touch.

While creatures actively interact with their environment with the help of their limbs, the *organs of sense* concentrated in the *head* do that in a more passive way. *Unrest* as a psychic quality, or tendency, listed in Figure 6 means that sensory impressions bring forth not only unrest, but also the *desire for perception*, which in some animals increases to a visible curiosity. That drive seems to be so strong in us that a total deprivation of environmental impulses will soon lead to psychic problems, as experiences with hospitalised children and test persons under extreme conditions such as isolation, silence and darkness show.

The brain, which works *analogous to* the computer, is strongly coupled with daily consciousness. We must consider the thinking sense as being the internal *sixth sense* in the centre of the five external senses. The *human activity* of *thinking* is even an extreme matrix of *unrest*. How much of that also applies to animals remains an open question. It is a fact that higher developed animals, such as the elephant, show an excellent memory. The ability to remember, however, can hardly be separated from the act of thinking, no matter how much animals differ from the intellect of *Homo sapiens* in that respect.

Four Life Circles of the Human Soul *analogous to* the Body

While the analogies of Figure 5 and Figure 6 apply to animals as well as to human beings, Figure 7, according to G R Heyer (14), emphasises the hierarchy of *creation*. All earthly life is based on *flora*, which made use of the four elements (soil, water, air, fire or radiation) and changed the surface of the earth in the beginning. The animals owe their power over plants to their *individual mobility*, which also shows in the constantly pumping heart. All animals depend directly or indirectly on flora, whose assimilation, growth and propagation have a continuing effect on animals and humans.

The *heart* serves as the engine of the *body machine*, since it keeps the *blood circulation* going throughout the whole body from birth to death. Blood mainly serves as a means of transportation for nutriments and waste substances, which is equal to the combined tasks of fresh water pipes and the sewage system. Furthermore, blood fulfils the same tasks as a postman *analogous to* the secretion of hormones. Blood circulation is closely connected to breathing, which corresponds to the location of the heart in the chest. The chest area is clearly separated from the stomach area by the diaphragm.

Life Circles of Physical Organisation according to G R Heyer, with Additional Remarks

Physical Area	Body Function	Realm of Creation	Distinguishing Attribute
head	sensory activities	realm of gods	(pure) consciousness
chest	breathing	human realm	activity of thinking
heart	blood circulation	animal realm	locomotion
belly	digestion	flora	growth

Figure 7

The separation by the *diaphragm* has a symbolic character since it separates the two lower realms of creation – plants and animals – from the upper two. The assignment of breathing (air element) to the *thinking ability* concurs with the medieval understanding of the four basic elements. If humans mainly distinguish themselves by their well-developed ability to think, the question remains what the sensory organs concentrated in the head (according to Figure 7) have to do with the highest realm of creation (gods). That question becomes more pressing today, since the lower kind of thinking (intellect) of modern man almost exclusively centres around *sensory impressions* and therefore – according to the Indian attitude – fulfils the task of a *sixth sense* within the *five* other senses.

We get a first indication from the *level* of the *sensory* organs in the head: while the *tongue* only responds to immediate stimulus, *nose* and *ears* receive messages from a greater distance. The *eyes* even penetrate immeasurable heavenly spaces, while they are greatly limited by almost all body types on earth.

Almost forgotten is telepathy, something man has in common with animals and plants. *Telepathy* does not only work passively like the other senses, but also *actively* in the transmission of *thoughts, feelings and imagery*. Since telepathy is not restricted to single sensory areas, as also applies to clairvoyance, etc., we can consider it to be a *universal sense*. Telepathy furthermore goes *beyond physical laws* such as electromagnetic radiation (light). Those characteristics place telepathy near pure consciousness, which is assigned to the realm of gods in Figure 7. How telepathy practically functions over a great distance is described in Figure (24) by two American researchers.

Is telepathy really so extraordinary that it has to be scientifically proven? Due to many daily experiences, the author is convinced that principally *every creature* has telepathic abilities. You only have to observe relevant experiences closely: did the ringing of the phone not make you immediately think of that person you had not heard of in a long time? More commonly, your partner unexpectedly expresses a thought you are pondering that very moment.

But even *animals and plants* are woven into that mysterious connection. When keeping that in mind, you will no longer wonder about 'tendencies as principles of creation' in Figure 8. Because tendencies in the author's meaning are the invisible, but highly effective, *drives of all creatures*.

Chapter III
THE SOUL OF ALL CREATURES AS A FORMATION OF TENDENCIES

The Universal Character of Tendencies

We can better understand the soul as an *energy complex* with its essential laws when we *generalise* the psychic drives as much as possible. As a side effect, we will discover certain factors they have in common with the lower realms of creation. The following Figure 8 is designed in such a way that the few basic tendencies of the *mineral* realm are put on the bottom, and the realms of *plants, animals* and *humans* rise in *growing abundance*. The effect of mineral tendencies reaches into the realm of humans, where they deserve closer observation as 'the power of habit'.

Tendencies as Principles of Creation

Human realm	curiosity and craving for knowledge, ability to order and organise, drives and interests, need to communicate, love and hate, ambition and vanity, arrogance and striving for power, abstinence and indulgence, Ego-consciousness and fear of death.
Realm of Animals	food and excretion, coupling and care in breeding time, drive to move and play, attack and defence (of territory), escape and playing dead, drive to control and herd instinct, sympathy and antipathy, memory and remembering, ability to learn, fright at death.
Realm of Plants ↑	growth and reproduction, maintenance and restoration, assimilation, striving to light and erection against gravity.
Realm of Minerals	*vis inertiae* and form stability

Figure 8

All *plant* tendencies also apply to animals and humans, such as the digestive processes (vegetative). All *animal* tendencies are found in human beings, which is indicated by many individuals having *animal names*. A few examples: Fox, Bird, Swan, Crow, Buck, Wolf. We find many characteristics among *humans* that otherwise only apply to certain animals. On the other hand, there are *typical human* characteristics such as *Ego-consciousness* that one looks for in vain among animals. The difference between human *fear* of *death* and animal *fright* at death is connected to that. Even love and hate are egocentric, while *sympathy* and *antipathy* occur in *all* realms, but are more obvious among animals than among plants.

Considering this multitude of creative powers, the author has defined tendencies in general as follows:

Tendencies = psychic-mental energies that determine the kind, direction and extent of all life processes

Figure 3

We often experience tendencies as being *inclined*, which is why they could also be called incliners and great tempters. That internal inclination corresponds to the *gradient* of *water* flowing into a valley, considering, however, only the *intensity* of the gradient. In reality, each body of flowing water also has a certain *direction*, as Figure 3 indicates *analogously* for tendencies. When we consciously strive for something, we talk about a goal we want to reach. When external obstacles or internal resistance in the form of *other tendencies* oppose a tendency, that tendency creates a corresponding need or feeling of *lacking*. Therefore, *Paul Debes* (10) calls tendencies 'starvelings'. A certain *tension* between desire and fulfilment even seems to be necessary for the health of an individual as well as of society.

Stability of Tendencies *analogous to* Inertia of Matter

It is a basic mechanical rule that every body on which *no* power pulls tries to maintain its position of rest, or the direction and speed of its movement. This *vis inertiae* is called inertia of matter possessed by every body, together with its gravity or weight. On a psychic level, the mechanical *vis inertiae* is equal to *habit*:

| habit of thinking, talking, acting and reacting | *analogous to* | *vis inertiae* of a body |

Figure 9

Habits can express themselves in *traditions* of dressing and rituals, in oral and written language, in rights and laws (customary law), as well as in all kinds of *dogmatism* (32). The fact that inveterate (incarnated) habits are based on the *energy* of *strong* tendencies only becomes apparent when there is a *change* in the usual rhythm due to external or internal disturbances. We can consider the constant *practice* and, more passively, the *adjustment* to new circumstances as a preliminary step to a habit. The German saying that constant 'practice makes a professional' does not only apply to skills in crafts and mental skills, but also applies to life in general. Through constant *repetition*, minimal beginnings can grow into mighty tendencies and habits that in the end happen automatically.

While the average person is exposed to that rule, the mentally ambitious know how to use it to his/her advantage. On the one hand, you have to patiently disassemble any *obstructive* habits through close observation of them and frequent pondering of their negative effects. On the other hand, you can create *new* habits that speed up your internal progress. The belief in one's own personality, the illusion of a self-separated 'I' from the world, stands out among habitual complexes. That *habitual* way of *thinking* nails us to the cross of the lower world and causes us to be *reborn* here and there according to the karmic law of mental causality.

Since a body rarely remains undisturbed, as presupposed in the analogy formula of Figure 9, we differentiate between two types of change in movement:

Change of the Activity of Tendency		Change of the Movement of Substance
increase (activation)	*analogous to*	acceleration (start)
decrease (passivation)		negative acceleration (braking)

Figure 10

We have seen that habits belong to the large group of *tendencies* that can only be observed when they show a certain activity. A fully passive tendency will, on principle, remain subconscious, no matter how strong it is.

With the aid of the simile of *flowing water*, we want to understand the *transition* of an active tendency to a passive condition. Since water always flows to deeper places available in its environment, rainwater in brooks and rivers will finally reach the ocean which offers the deepest level. Here, the flowing movement of the water stops, since all over the earth the sea level is in balance with local gravity. (The large ocean currents are caused by constant winds and differences in water temperature and salt content.)

activity of a tendency passivity of a tendency	*analogous to*	downwards (flowing water) entering the ocean

Figure 11

An old German folk song says that 'wandering is the miller's lust'. The analogy to a roaring stream propelling the mill is obvious. We remember the travelling artisans who swarmed out to the country in the early twentieth century to expand their trade skills. The drive to wander around is a tendency found in both humans and animals, which is why some people are called 'birds of passage'. Today's drivers and flying tourists seem to respond to the same urge to wander. B Chatwin (5) sees remains of the original nomad life in the unrest of our contemporaries. In the following formula, two levels are distinguished in analogy to the wind:

general drive to wander around (nomad way of life) periodical wandering (seasonal workers)	*analogous to*	irregular winds seasonal winds

Figure 12

Acceleration and negative acceleration of a *vehicle*, according to Figure 10, may lead us to the mechanical law of *reciprocal effect*, which remains hidden from the superficial view. You can push a vehicle on a dry, level road, something not possible to do on an icy surface, because the resistance to your feet on the road is missing. The pulling power of a locomotive with which it pulls the attached wagons works the same way, but in the opposite direction of the wagons to the engine. That applies under all conditions when we observe that, during braking, the pressure is transmitted via the buffers. While the counter-effect at the firing of a weapon is common knowledge, other effects of this kind, such as when firing a rocket or the dynamic lift of the wings, are only known to the expert.

Newton defined the law of reciprocal effect in the Latin form of '*actio = reactio*':

reaction to all actions (mental karmic law)	*analogous to*	effect = counter-effect (mechanical reciprocal effect)

Figure 13

The *karmic* law on the reaction to all egocentric, i.e., self-centred actions, goes far beyond the echo effect between humans. According to the Jewish rule, 'an eye for an eye, a tooth for a tooth', hate is automatically answered by hate, aggression by aggression. Since, on principle, all creatures strive for *pleasant encounters*, the sensible person has to *turn* the attitude, 'the way you treat me is the way I will treat you' into its *opposite*: 'the way I treat you is the way you will treat me'. When you surprise your partner with friendliness and understanding, s/he will at first react with *distrust*, since one does not want to believe such a change of attitude. *Mahatma Gandhi* and *Martin Luther King* with their great patience and a heart free of an ego were able to dissolve deep-rooted prejudices (habits of thinking) in the end. Their violent end is an indication of the delayed effects of the karmic law.

The basic law of human interrelations in the smallest group as well as on its highest level can generally be formulated as follows:

kind of encounter	amplification of similar *corresponds to* diminution of opposite	tendencies of partner

Figure 14

Instead of a description of condition by reading '*corresponds to*' as 'is *analogous to*', it is better to read the above formula as follows: the corresponding tendency change of the partner follows from the type of encounter. *Understanding* attention will *strengthen* similar tendencies within the partner, even if they remain hidden for a while. At the same time, *egocentric* and vengeful tendencies are *weakened*. Such *opposite* tendency couples, such as activity and want of rest, which can be found in everybody's heart, *do not extinguish* each other as water extinguishes fire, but appear individually under different circumstances.

Because of the law expressed by Figure 14, the *selection* of our *friends* is decisive for our passage through life, as long as we do not identify friends with drinking buddies and co-workers, blood relatives and neighbours, but rather *mental relatives*. Only these are models who will lift us morally and mentally according to the saying,

'Tell me who you socialise with,
and I will tell you who you are.'

A free-swinging pendulum is an evident illustration for the *preservation* of material *energy*. Without energy supply, it can carry out at least 1000 vibrations. If we pushed a pendulum freely suspended in a room void of air, it could theoretically swing forever. The most interesting aspect of a pendulum is the constant change between *potential* energy and *speed* energy. Let us try to put the *top* position of the pendulum, in which it remains *still* for a moment, *analogous to* the *appearance* of a *tendency* in our *daily consciousness*, before that tendency is suppressed below level by others. Then almost the whole distance the pendulum travels while swinging corresponds to the *subconscious* tendency condition. Hereby, however, the tendencies – *analogous to* the speed of the pendulum – are no less active than during the moments of consciousness:

Degree of Consciousness		Condition of Pendulum
consciousness of a tendency	*analogous to*	standstill on top
subconsciousness of a tendency		swinging back and forth

Figure 15

The same way as the total energy of the pendulum – which is its changing height and speed combined – remains constant, the tendency intensity stays the same – *independent* of its *degree* of consciousness (Figure 15) and its activity (Figure 10). However, we have to count on *slow* tendency *changes*, be it under the influence of people around us (Figure 14) or through internal work on the mental path.

Upon what *psychological* conditions does it depend whether a tendency quickly becomes subconscious again or remains conscious for a longer period of time? We know that, when conditions remain the same, habits of behaviour that take on an *automatic* character, i.e., become subconscious after a while, form easily. That applies to our perception, which can lead to *mental blindness* at the workplace and at home. Getting used to each other in a marriage often leads to mutual *indifference*. The unquestioned *fulfilment* of all physical needs such as clothing, food and the sexual act contribute to that phenomenon, which shall be generally formulated as follows:

regular and easy satisfaction	→	tendency becomes subconscious
irregular and difficult satisfaction	→	tendency remains conscious

Figure 16

You can observe that difference on all levels within yourself and others. The first line corresponds to the 'animal of habit' that we have already examined subsequent to the analogy in Figure 9.

Hierarchy of Tendencies *analogous to* the Hierarchy of a People

The same way that the *soul* within the trinity of
body–soul–mind
depicts a person's *energy*, the *people* are the *driving force* of a nation within the corresponding trinity of
country–people–government.
Therefore, you can consider soul and people as being analogous here, the analogy of which the author has individually substantiated in *Analogik Band 2* in a row of subgroups.

On the one side, it is clear that a nation consists of many individuals we call fellow citizens. On the other side, you can assume in theory that the partly subconscious tendencies consist of tiny energy particles, elementary tendencies or tendency atoms. The same way as material atoms can only be made visible in exceptional cases, tendency atoms or elementary tendencies are much too weak to become conscious. We treat the tendencies in the same way that a chemical scientist deducts individual atoms from the characteristics of a pure substance and ascribes certain characteristics to them, in analogy to a fellow citizen (Figure 17).

Pole reversals between love and hate that tend to revert to the opposite among passionate persons are especially striking.

Elementary Tendency		Fellow Citizen
intensity and direction		wealth and profession
type (quality)		race, type
pole reversal	*analogous to*	change of nationality
appearance and disappearance		birth and death

Figure 17

The appearance and disappearance of tendencies becomes more apparent if we differentiate between *four states* according to the following table:

State of an Elementary Tendency (on earth)		Soul of a Fellow Citizen
activity		embodied on earth
transition into the passive state	*analogous to*	passing away from earth
passivity		in the other world
transition into the active state		rebirth on earth

Figure 18

The terrestrial *death* of a fellow citizen corresponds to the *disappearance* of an elementary tendency, i.e., its *transition* from the active to the *passive* state. That passive state corresponds to the *other worldly* existence of a fellow citizen, who lost his influence on worldly society, but (as a soul) will be as active as he was on earth. The *return* of the fellow citizen to earth (physical rebirth) finally corresponds to the appearance and *reactivation* of the tendency, whose energy cannot just dissolve into nothing. It is common for a soul to embody itself repeatedly in the same nation.

In order to understand the aforementioned activity of the soul in the other world, we need the *opposite viewpoint* of Figure 18, i.e., the view from the other world on to earth. For that, we have to supplement the 'tendency aimed on the earth' in accordance with Figure 18 with a tendency aimed at the other world, and reverse the statements on the soul of a fellow citizen on the right side, as shown in the figure that follows:

State of an Elementary Tendency (aimed at the other world)		Soul of a Fellow Citizen
activity		embodied in the other world
transition into the passive state	*analogous to*	departure from the other world
passivity		on earth
transition into the active state		reappearance in the other world

Figure 19

The opposite side of death and birth indicated here becomes even more clear in Figure 69 (p. 81).

It is a rule of nature that *similar* forces and creatures *attract* each other, and dissimilar ones repel each other or remain indifferent to each other. That is why we can expect that similar elementary tendencies cluster into a tendency *cell*, the same way as a chemical *molecule* forms out of two or more atoms. Isolated atoms appear in nature as rarely as elementary tendencies. On a social level, several citizens form a *family*, and whole families are connected in a similar way. Each type of *relation* means a corresponding similarity. We can now put the two chains of similarities into the form of an analogy table:

elementary tendency		citizen
tendency cell	*analogous to*	family
tendency group		tribe
tendency complex		people of a nation

Figure 20

The same way that a family is more than the sum of its members, a molecule works completely differently from the mixture of its atomic particles. In both cases, the difference consists of the *powers* of *reciprocal effect* (Figure 13) between the members grown together. Even if a family as a 'cell of the nation' appears as a whole unit, its stability in today's industrial nations is far weaker than a few generations ago.

The attitude of society and government towards the family is subject to strong changes. Depending on the cultural, religious and political conditions of a nation, small families have been preferred over large families and vice versa. Today's urgent task of the developing countries is a strict *limitation* of the number of *children* in order to stop an explosive growth in population, before the nations tear each other apart in a worldwide catastrophe of starvation. *China*, with its population of over one billion, has actually succeeded in restricting the number of children born to each family in urban areas to one or two, a limitation that cannot be realised as quickly among its 800 million country residents.

A multitude of combined tendency cells should be considered as part of the tendency groups listed in Figure 20, the same way as many cells form one organ on a physical level. On the other hand, there are only a few homogeneous peoples. Most peoples consist of clearly distinguishable tribes, with their own family trees and histories. It is astonishing how even *smaller tribes* have been able to maintain their cultural individuality in dialect and traditions for centuries, something which is getting more and more difficult in modern times.

Even in old nations such as Great Britain, the hidden tensions between the tribes can rise to the surface for meaningless reasons and can give the government problems. These *tribal forces* are met by several countries by granting greater self-governing powers. In 1978, the separatist powers in the north of Canton Bern, Switzerland, were able to found an *independent* Canton Jura. Surprisingly, the Soviet Union broke up into its separate republics, among which the rivalries soon erupted openly. Yugoslavia followed that example; Serbian nationalism grew into a war of extermination against inconvenient minorities.

When talking of population, one mainly pictures the number of citizens, be it in the city or in rural areas. A population can increase or decrease for a variety of reasons. The analogy of Figure 18 can be generalised as follows:

Change of Tendency		Change in Population
strengthening of tendencies	*analogous to*	increase due to surplus of births
weakening of tendencies		decrease due to starvation, diseases, war

Figure 21

The *explosive increase* in population that many countries experience does not only lead to growing difficulties in supply but also to increased social tensions. On a psychological level, that corresponds to a difficulty in satisfying overpowering tendencies that enslave us:

overpowering activity of tendencies (difficult satisfaction)	*analogous to*	overpopulation of a country (difficult supply)

Figure 22

The same way that each nation should limit its population to a 'sensible number', we should strive for a healthy *balance* of our tendency household. The size of the population a country can feed and employ is a question of its level of development.

A population density that is too high forces the citizens to *emigrate*. In connection with catastrophes, it can cause whole migrations of nations. On the other hand, the population of the USA mainly grew out of European immigrants. Here, too, we have corresponding changes in tendencies:

Change in Tendency Group		Change in Size of Population
combination of similar tendency groups	*analogous to*	increase through assimilation of other tribes
separation of dissimilar tendencies from a group		decrease through emigration

Figure 23

While, in general, the grouping of tendencies occurs automatically according to the degree of similarity, combinations of apparently dissimilar tendencies can occur under special circumstances. When such a tendency group is only loosely connected to the other tendencies and expresses itself again and again in a certain manner, it is called a *complex*, according to C G *Jung*. Through repeated occurrence and an automatic course (compulsive act), it can reach such stability that you may suffer from it but can no longer get rid of it by yourself.

When psychology rediscovered the subconsciousness, it had to encounter suppressed energies of the soul. *S Freud's* pioneer work in that field is well known, but *sexuality* forms only one of the many tendency groups that are sometimes suppressed from daily consciousness. On principal, not all kinds of tendencies can be consciously realised simultaneously as long as you insist on your limited viewpoint of the self.

The rule that almost all nations have minorities who lead a restricted life and are often suppressed by the majority applies correspondingly:

suppressed tendencies	*analogous to*	minority, suppressed group

Figure 24

The minority may remain on the margin of society for reasons of race, language, religion or for any other reason. However, when the minority consists of a thin upper crust of discoverers, it will sooner or later succumb to the majority. We can then expect that masters and slaves *change roles*, which corresponds to the change between conscious and subconscious tendency groups found in a person.

The psychology of the *subconsciousness* teaches us that subconscious tendencies, be they suppressed or without ever having been conscious, can be extremely effective in the life of that person. Because of the great variety of tendencies, which surpasses anything imaginable, we have to assume really *passive* tendencies in each human being. In the course of incarnations, activity and passivity of many tendencies change, since each level of being encourages the activity of certain tendencies, while it condemns other tendencies to passivity, because they find no echo.

What does the *activity* of tendencies mean? That they have an effect on your life, which is connected to your environment by countless threads. Part of those are our human or social relationships, which are influenced by our personal development. Even though, on the other hand, a passive tendency will remain constant in its direction and intensity, this is not true for every active tendency. Because every action of thinking, talking or doing, and each reaction of approval or rejection will, due to the position it takes, lead to a slight change in the tendency:

| active/passive tendencies | *analogous to* | social/unsocial persons |

Figure 25

If active tendencies equal social persons, we have to assign the opposite type of person to the *passive* tendencies: unsocial persons, secretive individuals, fantasts, as well as monk-like hermits – in short, all those who are isolated from human contact for a lengthy period of time. Unsocial must clearly be differentiated from antisocial, a term of extremely negative character. The *unsocial* does not care about society, while the *antisocial* relates to society, but at the same time abuses it for immoral motives, or attempts to destroy it as a terrorist.

Individual Tendency Formation *analogous to* the Texture of a Rope

The expression 'individuality' stems from Latin, and means indivisibility. Individuality is a *unique* mental characteristic of which there are *no copies*. The analogy is taken from Figure 1 and amended:

mind. soul	*analogous to*	information energy	lame seer blind giant

Figure 26

This indicates memory and remembering as pillars of the mind. Another indication is the joint consciousness: a being's internal *connection* with all *creatures*. In Christianity, this is called *altruism*, and in Buddhism it is called *all-love* (*metta*): a love which does not differentiate between the self and another being.

With individuality comes the curious talent that all of its actions and *experiences* – be they of a high or a low quality – are *stored* as in a computer and, at the point of a certain development, can be *recalled from the past*, no matter how far away. That automatic 'writing down' is called *acasha chronicle* in India; in the Bible it is called *Book of Life*. The remembering of earlier incarnations (one's own and others') proves the *indestructible tie* that connects all our incarnations like a *chain of pearls*. The tendency network of the soul has the same characteristic of constancy, or *continuity*.

As the right column of Figure 27 shows, with the old parable of the blind giant and the lame seer, they both depend on each other inseparably:

the blind giant the lame seer	*analogous to*	the soul, is lost without his leader the mind, cannot move without his carrier

Figure 27

Accordingly, we must assume that the mental tie of individuality, which we have set into analogy to a chain of pearls, is inseparably connected to the rope texture still to be discussed.

If we consider individuality to be the *highest level* of the mind, we can add two lower levels to it, which we set into analogy to three consistencies of a crystal:

Mind		Crystal
individuality		shape as mental image
self	*analogous to*	liquid crystal
Ego		solid crystal

Figure 28

Let us start with the bottom line, our *Ego-consciousness*. It *considers* itself as being *separated* from the rest of creation because it *identifies* itself with the *mortal body*. Only mentally striving persons experience how fiercely the Ego defends its position. On your painful way to the lonely top, a more extensive psychological instance is developed, which *C G Jung* called the *Self*. Contrary to the Ego, the Self knows *no* tendency for power and *no* boundary between mine and yours. The relationship between the Ego and the Self is *analogous to* that between a solid and a *liquid* crystal, in accordance with Figure 28. Only the Ego, *analogous to* a solid crystal, is familiar to us. But even a liquid crystal has its *invisible* crystal *axis* with curious *optical characteristics*. We can view these axes as mental images of a certain crystal shape, which corresponds to mental *individuality*.

The question may arise as to whether there are also other individual tendency network souls? The *group souls* of animal species and human masses, on which mass psychology concentrates, can be found among these. The souls of the individual *animals* belonging to one species are *closely connected* to the group soul, as we can observe in a swarm of mosquitoes dancing up and down. *Humans* and higher beings such as *angels* and *gods*, on the other hand, possess individual souls that are only *loosely* connected with other beings and groups.

The analogies of Figure 18 to Figure 20 already mentioned elementary tendencies, which are much too weak to become conscious when isolated. A fitting simile to *elementary* tendencies is offered by *natural fibres* that are spun into a *thread*. This corresponds to a group of very similar elementary tendencies that, due to their similarity, settle closely together. A series of threads is twisted into a *rope*, and a thick *cable* can be made out of several ropes. Accordingly, we can picture the structure of a tendency formation:

Structure of a Tendency Formation		Rope Structure
elementary tendency		single fibre
group of similar elementary tendencies	*analogous to*	thread spun out of fibres
main group of tendencies belonging together		rope twisted out of fibres
whole tendency formation		cable made of rope

Figure 29

At each cross-cut of a thick cable, only a tiny section of all fibres are on the *surface*. They equal those tendencies that surface to *consciousness* for reason of their *activities*, while the major part of the tendencies *remains passive*. Since the single fibres are a lot *shorter* than the structure made from them, we can assign the *beginning* of a fibre to the formation of an elementary tendency, and the *end* of the fibre to the *dissolution* of that tendency:

formation dissolution	of an elementary tendency	*analogous to*	beginning end	of a fibre

Figure 30

The *formation* of a tendency occurs through the strict *affirmation* of a matter, quality, activity or condition. A *weak* tendency, on the other hand, can be *totally dissolved* through strict negation, as we will see in Section 5 of Chapter VI: 'The Rule of Tendency Changes'. Of course, that process takes longer for stronger tendencies.

The one end of the 'tendency cable' reaches into the past to lose itself before the eye of a seer in the times gone by – 'appearances and disappearances of worlds' – an image often used by *Buddha* in connection with reincarnation. The other end of the tendency cable is formed by the present and the near future, in which 'the norns spin the thread of fate'. The *thread of fate* serves as an ancient simile, as is indicated in the expression 'your fate hangs on a single thread'.

You probably noticed the words 'elementary tendencies' on the left side of the analogy table (Figure 20) as well as under the title of the formula of Figure 29. That enables you to form the *analogy chain*:

| citizen | *analogous to* | elementary tendency | *analogous to* | single fibre |

which also results in the analogy between the two *final links*:
| citizen | *analogous to* | single fibre |

Accordingly, you will see:
| people | *analogous to* | cable |

for the corresponding overall qualities. That means, illustratively: the stream of heritage as a result of generations corresponds to the special order of the multiple short fibres in the long thick cable.

Humanity *analogous to* Fabric

At first, the basic connection between similarity and special closeness, which depicts a very close analogy, is formulated as follows:

| *degree* of similarity and analogy (quality) | *analogous to* | special closeness (quantity $1/r^2$) |

Figure 31

As an expression of *closeness*, one could insert the reciprocal value $1/r$ of the *distance* r between the *things observed*. Since most physical effects such as light, sound and gravity *decrease* from their source in accordance with r^2, Figure 31 shows the square reciprocal value of the distance $1/r^2$. With the help of that analogy, the world of space in which all earthly things have their home is put in relation to the world of psychic-mental qualities. This is shown even more clearly in the third rule, 'similarity and analogy mean attraction to and effect on each other' (7), since attraction and intensity of radiation increase with closeness ($1/r^2$).

This connection (Figure 31) is fulfilled in the next *other world* (*astral* level) through the fact that the souls are compellingly *attracted* to those societies and external conditions that are *most similar* to their moral qualities. On earth, we often miss those similarities when we meet spouses who, on a psychological level, do not match at all, in spite of the fact that they have to get along very closely. In those cases, a look back to *earlier incarnations* of both spouses would give us clarity about their karmic entanglements, which can now be dissolved with the right insight. This is also the reason for distinct reactions between apparent strangers who meet for the first time on earth and feel 'love at first sight' for each other – or the opposite: an inexplicable strong antipathy and fear.

Those psychological ties that work subconsciously encompass a wide range of possibilities: *threads* of sympathy and love, but also threads of antipathy or hate run between the individual tendency formations of the souls in accordance with Figure 29. Even though such *negative* connections are experienced as being repelling, antipathy, disgust and hate form just as strong tendency *bonds* as the positive connections. This is a much overlooked psychological rule, as *Shaw Desmond* has convincingly illustrated by numerous examples in *Love after Death* (11).

Strong connections between humans require a series of incarnations for their development, and develop further on higher levels of being. On the other hand, the psychic-mental energy invested by both parties cannot just disappear. That is the reason why, even in the future, the *destinies* of such souls are mysteriously connected for a while.

While strong psychic bonds are rather the exception, the medium-strong connections to our friends and acquaintances, to whom we feel more or less connected, are rather common. In addition, there are personalities from many different countries with whom the media acquaints us. The steadily growing masses of refugees lets us sympathise with the fate of *groups* of people that would otherwise have remained strangers to us. With that, the cable structure of the individual tendency formation (Figure 29) expands into a living *fabric* (Figure 32), in which we can picture the tendency cables to lie rather parallel, whereby those *most similar* lie next to each other.

The analogy to a simple fabric, such as used to be created on countless looms in private households, is suitable. The *warp* threads lying closely next to each other form the carrying structure in the long direction of the fabric. The shuttle 'shoots' the *woof* thread back and forth, which constantly creates new connections between the warps. This obviously corresponds to connections between humans:

Fabric on Earth		Simple Textile Fabric
tendency cables connections between humans	analogous to	layer of warp thread result of woof thread

Figure 32

The *manual* loom was the model for the first *power* looms, which worked considerably faster and caused many weavers to become unemployed. Nowadays, there are even specialised power looms that can create thicker fabrics with the help of several warp systems. For that effect, several woofs are used, some of which run transversal through a layer of warps, while others run vertically. This makes considerable expansion possible:

Tendency Fabric on Several Levels of Being		Multilayered Fabric
tendency cables on several levels of being connections between humans on and between several levels of being	analogous to	several layers of warp threads several woof threads

Figure 33

Such three-dimensional fabric by far exceeds the simple two-dimensional fabric, in accordance with Figure 32. *Analogously*, we are not only connected to the six billion humans living on earth today but, according to (1), also to a group of sixty billion souls that partake in eternal wanderings through high and low, light and darkness, heaven and hell in refined and rougher embodiments. *Buddha* points out that we have been related to all other human souls in the course of innumerable incarnations, be it on a physical or a psychic-spiritual level, and that the knowledge of this should be an incentive to us to practise all-love (*metta*).

How can the qualitative division of the *levels of being* be put into relation with the multilayered fabric (Figure 33)? Several layers of warp threads are required for its production, which are at first separated as neatly in the power loom as the levels of being in Figure 51. In the finished three-dimensional fabric, however, they are woven together as tightly as the levels of being with their vibrations, according to parapsychology.

Furthermore, we want to picture that the *most* active *tendency* ropes within a tendency cable (Figure 29) *stand out* from the less active or even completely passive tendencies. According to the Rule of Similarity (Figure 31), those most active tendencies of a being are automatically pulled on to the analogous level of being: the cause for the next incorporation, be it on earth or in another, more refined world.

Since every incarnated being belongs to a *group* of souls, the *analogies* of *connections* between humans come into play. They represent the woof threads of a fabric (Figure 32). The same way as these hold the warp threads together, the *social instincts* are the *glue* that keep the sixty billion souls invisibly, but effectively, together. However, we should never imagine that psychological 'glue' as a static power, but rather as a highly *dynamic* process – *analogous to* the exchange forces in the science of nuclear physics. The Indians call that eternal process of birth, aging and dying 'Samsara', which is known in Europe as Wheel of Rebirths.

Our psychologists use the rather careful term of 'collective subconsciousness'. As an illustration, the simile of the *iceberg* is often used, whereby the visible tip of a swimming iceberg represents the consciousness, and the larger part under water represents the subconsciousness. This simile can be formulated more exactly on four levels (Figure 34).

The two centre lines describe the personality *analogous to* the iceberg. The surrounding *sea water* covers seventy per cent of the surface of the earth and *connects* all icebergs with each other. Correspondingly, all of the sixty billion human souls – and moreover all other creatures – are connected through the *collective* subconsciousness. The iceberg, however, is not just being moved by currents but also by winds. The surrounding *atmosphere* corresponds to the *super*consciousness, which reaches beyond the I and the you, time and space, and 'transcends' this world. This *spiritual* aspect is too often forgotten.

Psychological Level		Swimming Iceberg
superconsciousness		surrounding atmosphere
day-consciousness	*analogous to*	visible tip
personal subconsciousness		part under water
collective subconsciousness		surrounding body of water

Figure 34

A religious person may supplement, as another level, in Figure 34:

God | *analogous to* | radiation from space

Figure 35

The esoteric considerations in this section will be continued in Chapter V (Embodiment and Re-Embodiment), Chapter VI (Immortality of the Soul as a Tendency Formation), and Chapter VII (Meditation as Mystical Solution for the Soul).

The following chapter, however, is mainly dedicated to the psychic-mental drives (tendencies) of the whole person, in analogy to special forms of energy. Thus, the author's method presented in the introduction – namely the consistent use of the rule of *energy preservation*, not only in the *external world* on earth, but also in the psychic *internal world* – is applied in individual steps.

Chapter IV
HUMAN TENDENCY GROUPS *ANALOGOUS TO* WORLDLY FORMS OF ENERGY

Person and Personality

Even though 'person' is a standard term, you may have difficulties in defining it. The author suggests the following definition:

Natural person = ensouled human body

Figure 36

The same way that a *natural* person is identified through his or her personal data, a *legal* person identifies a society or company that can legally act like a single person. From the *official point* of view, a new person enters this world at each birth, but that is different from the *psychological* point of view: as long as a toddler speaks of himself or herself in the third person, using his or her first name, he or she is still living in the *magic age* of our forefathers, who knew no persons of today's meaning.

Only at the very moment when a child follows the example of adults and says 'I', has he *separated* from the union with all beings and *faces* the world as an *individual* person. Psychologically, that is the birth of a new person who will *die* at the point of earthly *death* (or soon thereafter). As long as you see yourself *exclusively* as a person, you *have to fear* death as destruction. All you can do is suppress the inevitable end from your consciousness.

At the same time, this indicates the *solution* to the dilemma of modern man: the *expansion* of the day consciousness beyond one's physical needs. This can be done in several ways. A few main points are:

1. Acceptance of the right of all people to satisfaction of their basic needs, such as food, shelter, education, work.
2. Acceptance of basic *freedom* – particularly for *minorities* – in regard to family, race, finances, faith, politics (practical tolerance).
3. In agreement with all major religious faiths, all wise men recommend *virtue* – not in order to please God or the Church, but to become fit *for life on* earth *and* in the *other* world. Irritations in human relationships can be limited to a minimum if we follow the general principle: don't do to others what you don't want done to yourself.
4. By realising this principle, more and more, and easier and easier will you notice a constant *improvement* of your *basic mood*, while your egocentric frustrations will slowly dissolve at the same time. As a result, you will become mentally and physically healthier.

Psychologically, that development means the expansion of a person to a personality:

Personality = self-assured part of our soul that is *independent* from the terrestrial body

Figure 37

The development of one's own personality is neither an issue of school education or knowledge, nor of profession or social standing. Personality should also not be mixed up with intellectual arrogance. On the contrary, the more *harmoniously* you develop, the more *modestly* you will face the world and the *less dependent* you will become on the dispersions of the external world. This '*self*-assured part of the soul' will certainly survive death on earth, no matter what the personality believes the other world to be.

The Ego-consciousness of a person who has left his or her worldly body can, on the other hand, follow the soul only into the *interregnum*, where the soul will stay full of earthly assumptions for a while. Here it must suffer a second death, namely, the death of its ego, before it can merge with the other souls on the astral level. The missing psychological development of a person (Figure 36) into a personality (Figure 37) can, therefore, be made up for in the other world – as long as the person is not a hardened materialist, whose 'psychological weight' will soon pull him or her out of the interregnum back into another birth on earth. We can assign the rigid person (most striking among older persons) to the *terrestrial* world and the more flexible personality to the *astral* world – see the two lowest lines of Figure 51.

In the following two sections, psychic drives of the personality are set analogously to different kinds of heat production, and in Section 3 of Chapter IV, mental drives follow *analogous to* radiation energy. Psychic and mental drives are among the great manifoldness of tendencies, of which Figure 8 offers a first overview.

Psychic Drives of the Personality *analogous to* Worldly Forms of Energy

MECHANICAL AND HEAT ENERGY (IN THE HOME)

Mechanical Energy

Indispensable mechanical energy is still available in developing countries in the form of millions of draught-animals. The same way as industrialisation was only enabled through the availability of *mechanical* energy, modern society is characterised by the striving for *personal* profit. Even communist countries can no longer ignore that tendency. Ego-emphasised striving appears in aspects such as greed for money and power, ambition and vanity, the mania to break records... these and many similar tendencies occur on the *surface* of personality and poison the social atmosphere of our planet. Accordingly, mechanical energy is one of the roughest forms:

| ego-emphasised striving | *analogous to* | mechanical energy |

Figure 38

Combustion Energy

Mechanical and electrical energy, as well as light – which will be considered later – change into heat even without our doing. Already in former times, people knew how to make fire out of heat produced by friction. Artificial fire can be considered the beginning of human culture, and fire through chemical burning has still kept its dominating position.

Most inhabitants of the earth still depend on *natural fuels* from their environment for preparation of their food on the open fire. On the other hand, industries use masses of coal, crude oil and natural gas: waste products of plant life, which nature has stored for us over millions of years. The *storage capacity* of chemical energy particularly distinguishes this form of energy, while heat energy quickly mingles with the colder surroundings and dissipates.

In order to find the psychic analogy to physical warmth, we think of a warm nest and a warm heart, to warm one's heart for something or someone, and then of the opposite. *E Swedenborg* occupies himself in detail with the analogy between warmth/heat and love. Have you noticed how the wind and cold seem to rebound from two people in love? Even more impressively, the great lovers of God prove that, in general:

| love is | *analogous to* | combustion heat |

Figure 39

whether this is illustrated by a yogi sitting naked in the snow or a holy man without food. Because food does not only create energy, but also heat. Another well known example is offered by the patron saint of Switzerland, *Niklaus von der Flüe*, who carried on his life of atonement for decades without taking in any food.

Open Fire

We want to differentiate four degrees of heat creation through burning. The corresponding quality of love has got a bad reputation through today's sex propaganda. Even though man has a sexual drive in common with animals, the physical attraction between two people can become a gateway to higher forms of love, to which *Paul* dedicates a hymn in the first Epistle to the Corinthians.

At first, we linger at the consuming physical desire that overcomes lovers like a blazing fire. That is the most popular subject among the masses. Undoubtedly, sexual love is one of the roughest forms, which is why we assign the most primitive heat production to it:

| Sexual love | *analogous to* | open fire |

Figure 40

Even though sexuality in *Freud*'s meaning had a more general connotation than nowadays, sexual love remains a non-lasting value. It is like a craved meal that satisfies for only a few hours. For many people, sexual love even takes on the character of a *product* that is *sold* to the highest bidder. 'Love for sale' is, strictly speaking, no love at all.

You may remember chemical analogies. The fusion of single atoms into stable molecules releases energy that can appear as combustion heat. Very similarly, the blazing up of a love affair is experienced as psychic energy set free, and that is the reason why many people keep looking for new lovers. Here, the *process* of *falling in love* is more important than the partner's personality.

Domestic Hearth

The domestic hearth was a first major step in controlling fire. During the long winter nights, the whole family used to gather around the heat-giving fireplace. In those 'good old days', people still had the time to tell fairy tales to children. The same way as the fire is tamed in the hearth, sexual love is tamed in a marriage, which *Friedrich Schiller* hints at in *Song Of The Bell*. A restriction of the analogy of Figure 40 is formulated as follows:

| marital love | *analogous to* | domestic hearth |

Figure 41

Marital love, in contrast to 'illicit love', plays a major role for *Swedenborg* (25).

It was only a few steps from one central hearth to several ovens in different rooms. In the country, there are still tiled stoves that store the heat for hours. Russian farmers used to have a giant tiled stove as a cosy sleeping place for the whole family, where they all gathered like groundhogs.

Central Heating

The ambitious industrial age aided the striving for comfort and economy, cleanliness and controllability by creating a central system for the different ovens distributed all over the house. The same way as smoke rises through the chimney, warm water rises in the central heating system and carries the heat to the individual radiators. Since this natural circulation (convection) takes place slowly and requires thick pipes, it is sped up by a *circulating pump, analogous to* the heart.

What does the distribution of heat by convection mean in regard to Figure 39? Obviously, that love expands to other family members, friends and co-workers. The circle of persons whose lives one actively takes part in and for whom one is ready to sacrifice something has expanded from the close family, but the circle of expansion is limited. Accordingly, the central heating system was, at first, limited to one-family *homes* or apartments:

love towards family and friends = central heating in the home or apartment

Figure 42

Today's technology has developed further and now one power plant heats whole parts of cities with hot water or steam, which carries the benefit of reduced pollution. According to Figure 39 – 'love *analogous to* combustion heat' – the expansion of the heating system corresponds to an expansion of love into general *altruism*. Altruism makes no distinction between natives or strangers, black or white, Moslem or Hindu. Different from Ego-centred love, altruism does *not expect gratitude*, but instead finds satisfaction when the advice or assistance offered to another person meets with success. Not to give charity, but rather to assist others in *helping themselves* – that must be the aim of economic aid, which has gone wrong so often in the past. We summarise:

altruism	*analogous to*	collective heating of whole city parts

Figure 43

OTHER METHODS OF HEAT PRODUCTION

Mechanically-Produced Heat

Besides heat production through combustion (oxidation), there are two other kinds of mechanical heat production. Probably the oldest method of making fire is to rub dry pieces of wood together until they ignite. This way, we can warm our cold hands. In technology, *frictional heat* is an undesired side effect: brake surfaces heat up when constantly used, a grinding coupling begins to stink, blocked train wheels create sparks.

From a *physical* point of view, *work* is required to create frictional heat. During any type of work, some kind of resistance that occurs along the way is overcome. Psychologically, this corresponds to the *internal* efforts we undertake each day, *apart* from pure muscle work. All intense psychic-mental processes, such as the solution of difficult tasks, tests of our patience, anger and disputes, can literally heat us up.

But even habitual mental work requires a minimum of attention and concentration. The energy consumed during that work shows in exhaustion. No matter what type of work we carry out, we can describe the psychic condition that best equals frictional heat with the following analogy:

| ambitious work | *analogous to* | frictional heat of a solid substance |

Figure 44

Frictional heat also exists in streaming *gases*. *Supersonic* aeroplanes heat up from air molecules flying by. Due to the air jam, the air at the leading edges of the plane heats up to a similar degree. This effect is so strong among the yet faster rockets and space missiles during their re-entry into the atmosphere that they *heat up red-hot*. It is known of *shooting stars* that they even evaporate when they pass through earth's atmosphere at a speed of ten to seventy kilometres per second. This is the way that our planet protects itself from a rain of cosmic projectiles, of which larger chunks only rarely reach the surface of the earth.

In order to find a psychological connection to the ways air heats up, as mentioned above, we remember the medieval equation of thinking to air quality. When we warm towards something and develop a *preference*, we are emotionally involved, which we can describe with the term *interest* to be there. How strongly we are bound by interests only becomes apparent when we are blocked by another party. A huge network of personal interests surrounds our globe. New conflicts, which can only rarely be solved by cold rationale, constantly ignite from that net of interests. Insofar, we are correct to amend the basic connection of Figure 39 – 'love *analogous to* combustion heat' – as follows:

Interest		Heating up through
theoretical	*analogous to*	gas condensation
practical		wall friction in gases

Figure 45

The air pump is an example of heating up through gas condensation. Considerably more is achieved by a diesel engine whose air inside the cylinder is condensed to about eighty atmospheres and therefore reaches the point of ignition of heavy oil. The fact that heating up also occurs during slower condensation is evidenced by sinking masses of air in a high pressure area that become a good degree drier at the same time, and bring good weather with them.

When a projectile hits a solid wall at high speed, its energy of movement turns into heat, which suffices to melt the projectile. To a lesser degree, this transformation is employed during forging, whereby the piece of iron is heated up further with each blow of the hammer. This is a good simile for a *blow of fate*, something each of us has probably already experienced personally, or in his/her environment. Blows of fate usually occur as losses, be it one's property, family members, home or health. A strange rule comes into effect here: the things we have lost, we appreciate the most. We often become aware of our love for a person with whom we lived in dispute for years only after we have lost him or her. In a similar way, our attitude towards our own body can change – as long as it serves its daily duty, we don't pay much attention to it; only to begin to love it when it requires care due to an accident or illness.

Since *longing* depicts a special kind of love, we put down as the second form of mechanically-produced heat:

longing for something suddenly lost (blow of fate)	*analogous to*	heating up through a blow or crash of projectile

Figure 46

The saying 'you first have to go away so you can come back home' clearly expresses *homesickness*, i.e., longing for a lost home. This homesickness can turn into an energy consuming all of terrestrial life, while our souls already lost their paradise on a higher level aeons ago.

Electric Heat

The most common method for changing electrical energy into heat is based on electrical *resistance*, known to us as metallic wire spirals. Inside radiators, they serve to directly heat the air, in stoves for cooking, and in hot-water boilers to utilise the cheaper night rates. In *electrolysis*, low-tension direct current is used, as in the separation of water into hydrogen and oxygen. During electrochemical processes, the created heat is an undesired side effect. For electrical *welding*, on the other hand, the development of heat in the arc between the electrode and the welded piece is required. Nature offers us such spectacular electric arcs in *lightning*.

The more we mentally return to former times, when travelling was primitive and dangerous, the more we wonder about the courageous predecessors of modern vagabonds. In the fates of discoverers of new countries, the *love of adventure* is the essential drive of their activities. We put that tendency in relation to heat produced by electricity:

Drive of Personality		Electric Heat through
love of adventure	*analogous to*	resistance
passion for discovery		induction

Figure 47

What good would the greatest love of adventure be to a human being if he did not have considerable physical and psychic health to successfully overcome any resistance? Many started out to have adventures, and only few of them returned unharmed.

In reference to heat production, it does not matter whether DC or AC flows through a rheostat. Only the alternating current, however, makes possible *magnetic transmission* of energy through *induction without directly* touching the circuits. That inductive coupling forms the basis of the small dimmer for light bulbs and of the large transformers for the adaptation of electrical voltage. The same principle of energy transmission serves in an induction furnace for melting metals that are not heated by a heating element but by electrical eddy currents.

According to previous analogies, the psychic mirror image of inductive electrical heat is associated with the *thirst for knowledge* and love. Picture a passionate scientist who will not give up until he has found the laws of nature or technical processes that he was looking for. He neither hesitates to risk his fortune nor to risk the loss of his good reputation, and is often considered crazy. In his extreme *love for the issue*, such a scientist even risks his health, as history has shown in several tragic examples. The second line of Figure 47 is meant in that sense – a dozen examples of 'psychic drives of personality'. The reader may supplement them with additional psychic energies, with analogies from his own experience.

Mental Drives of Personality *analogous to* Radiation Energy

THE COLLABORATION OF SOUL AND MIND

In Figure 1, we touched on the subject of soul and mind within the framework of the traditional trinity. With the help of a rather general tendency definition (Figure 3), you could familiarise yourself with the idea of 'the soul as a transworldly energy complex'.

On the other hand, the 'mind' is closely connected to consciousness and memory. This ability to store impressions can be retraced all the way to simple dead matter. Soul and mind are similar insofar as the psychic energy is stored in the tendencies, and the mental contents in the memory.

Nowadays, consciousness is only considered in connection with knowledge and information. However, even the most primitive *day-*consciousness would be impossible without a subtle *background* consciousness, which accordingly applies to dream consciousness. We want to clarify this with a film analogy:

Consciousness and Tendencies		Film Theatre
background consciousness		white screen
day-consciousness	*analogous to*	projected film images
change of conscious condition		change of film roll
active tendencies		cinema goers

Figure 48

The cinema goers only start to look up when the projector throws film images on the empty screen. After the main film has begun, you will soon forget the screen itself. The *identification* of the audience with the movie stars and their adventures sometimes even lets the viewers forget that they are in a cinema. On a psychological level, the average person reacts similarly during the course of the day: they *identify* with their *sensual* impressions (I see and I think). That day-consciousness is shut off during the process of falling asleep, *analogous to* the end of the film. *Dream* consciousness equals the playing of *another* film.

Insofar, the three subgroups of Figure 48 may be illuminated. However, since no film is shown without an audience, the question of an analogy to the *cinema goers* arises. They are a person's *active tendencies*, without which no day-consciousness can occur. The background consciousness, however, remains even when no tendencies are active or – more rarely – when all tendencies are dissolved.

We return to the ancient simile for the close relationship between the soul and the mind in Figure 27, whereby we have to imagine that the blind giant carries the lame seer on his shoulders:

| mind | | lame seer |
| soul | *analogous to* | blind giant |

Figure 49

The image of the *blind giant* excellently corresponds to the *soul* as a tendency formation, or energy complex, in the sense in which the author sees the soul. The *lame seer*, *analogous to* the mind, has no power to walk, but a good general view to show the blind giant the way.

If the lame seer has healthy senses but is *enslaved* to the blind giant, he will try to satisfy the momentary desires of his carrier by showing him respective ways. This is difficult, however: firstly, those desires often change, and secondly they are so varied that it would be almost impossible to satisfy three or four wishes at the same time, which is why most of the giant's *desires* must remain *unfulfilled*. This paradoxical, but suitable image depicts modern man, who tries at all costs to satisfy his needs in this world.

As the other extreme of this dissimilar couple, let us imagine that the *lame seer* has the mental qualities of a *wise man*. With these qualities, he cannot only show the main direction of their long march, but also steer the giant's next steps in a way that both benefit from. This means patiently supporting the *healthy* tendencies and weakening the unhealthy. On the road to healing, transmitted from wise men, we pay more and more attention to the laws of *virtue*, which improves our relationships with other humans. It is also healing to limit one's own needs, because that strengthens one's independence, while a society of consumers leads to material slavery.

The above simile indicates the strong *reciprocal effect* between soul and mind. A mentally striving person must use this effect wisely if s/he wants to solve his/her entanglements with the terrestrial (or astral) world and end the painful process of endless rebirths. The author points out the clearly written exposition by *P Debes* (10) to those who are interested in this way, described in detail by *Buddha*.

There is *no basic difference* between the *psychic* drives previously described and the *mental* drives to be described in the following passages. They all belong to tendencies, or transworldly energies. The differentiation between terms of psychic and mental drives has a mere practical meaning. Mental drives, or tendencies, are *created by thoughts* that have been often repeated and therefore become a habit. That is the reason why habits, just as inherent personality traits, belong to the pure tendency energies that are aimed at a particular goal, which can be active or passive. *R Sheldrake* (23) comes to similar conclusions with his concept of 'morphogenetic fields'.

EGO-EMPHASISED STRIVING *ANALOGOUS TO* RADIATION OF PARTICLES

Emitted rays such as light or radiation beams are electromagnetic *waves*, to which radio waves also belong, only their waves are considerably longer. Recently, physicists have also assigned physical characteristics to all those kinds of waves that speed through space at light velocity (zero-mass photons). *Particle* radiation, on the other hand, consists of a stream of particles such as atoms and their components. A *rain shower* offers a good simile for particle radiation such as that which the sun continuously sends out into space, besides waves of light.

As an analogy for invisible atomic particles on a *psychological* level, we have the Ego that experiences itself only as a meaningless grain of sand in a mass of people. This *passive* aspect of the average person particularly occurs in large cities with millions of inhabitants, the growth of which is increasing to a shocking extent. The civilised person experiences the *active* aspect when he or she is moving in the stream of believers of progress towards an imaginary goal, which they will never reach due to the obvious destruction of their home planet. Isn't the simile of particle radiation obvious here?

The Ego is no independent centre, in spite of the fact that even unimportant individuals feel this way at happy moments. The simile of an inconsistent dewdrop, with the following three subgroups, is more fitting:

Ego as Personal Centre		Dewdrop
awakening in childhood		creation and enlargement through condensation
fast-changing aspects	*analogous to*	glittering in the sun
dissolution through earthly death		minimalisation and dissolution through evaporation

Figure 50

That inconsistency of the Ego stems from identification with constantly new tendencies (Figure 3), which temporarily pass into the consciousness and submerge again, almost unchanged, in order to make room for other tendencies. The iridescence of a glittering dewdrop contradicts its relative consistency as little as the changing positions of the Ego-centre contradict the 'consistency of tendencies' that form the cause of the psychological spectacle of an Ego.

The Ego-emphasised striving of our civilisation can take on a variety of shapes. A striking example is *ambition*, which most societies consider to be a healthy characteristic, at least in males. It corresponds to female *vanity*. Certainly, there are also vain men and ambitious women, since all character features are distributed to both sexes, even with a difference in frequency. A strong group of *Ego-emphasised* characteristics can be circumscribed with arrogance, pride, conceit and the opposite. Such an Ego-consciousness may be based on birth and property, social status and title, skills and knowledge. These more collective character features seem to lack striving, which appears, however, the very moment their usual social status is questioned. Therefore, these are also tendencies.

Another, probably just as widespread group emphasises the social character as opposed to egocentric characteristics. Undoubtedly, it is not difficult to recognise the uncountable forms of *practical altruism*, all the way to female willingness to sacrifice everything (for a man) (19). But, in most cases, it is easy to discover, behind social activities, the *personal striving* that endeavours to find satisfaction in acknowledgement, silent power and success. A different, *superpersonal* kind of striving is extremely rare, since it requires a very high moral-mental level.

PROSELYTISM *ANALOGOUS TO* HEAT RADIATION

With heat radiation, we supplement the analogies to combustion heat (Figure 39) and electric heat (Figure 47). Every glowing object radiates heat and light. But heat can be felt far below 100°C, a fact utilised in ceiling heater systems, where the heat spreads throughout the whole room and even warms up the floor, while an open fire mainly heats its immediate surroundings.

The sun was the first source of radiation for man and is therefore desired and admired in a cold climate, while inhabitants of tropical countries prefer the shade. Did you as a child also try to set a piece of paper on fire with the help of a magnifying glass? The *concentration* of sunbeams through a mirror is utilised more and more, whether with a tin mirror under an Indian cooking pot or complicated mirror sections for the intensification of radiation by 1,000 times, whereby temperatures of over 3,000°C are reached.

Luminous radiation is virtually imponderable and appears to be the opposite of all solid material. Radiation must, therefore, be equal to the highest principle of human intelligence, namely to *ideas*, in the sense of *Plato*. Since heat is *analogous to* love, we can assign heat radiation to the love of particular ideas. This includes people who identify with an idea and feel forced to make others happy with it: inventors, social reformers, public speakers, preachers and missionaries. They all have *proselytism* in common, which can get as extreme as fanaticism.

INTELLECT, LOGIC AND SPECULATION *ANALOGOUS TO* VISIBLE LIGHT

While the sun sends us perceptible heat and visible light, we can only see the light of moon and stars. This light has always curiously attracted *humans*. Isn't it strange that *animals* are indifferent to the sight of moon and stars, even though they have an excellent ability to observe?

A greater improvement than electric light, with which we make day out of night, was probably the invention of *window glass*. It offered larger windows through which daylight could enter rooms even during the cold season. Before that, the openings of houses had to be stuffed in winter.

The 'light of perception' symbolically indicates that we mainly perceive the terrestrial world through our eyes, which are directed towards the front, while the eyes of animals – with a few exceptions – are directed sideways. This suits our 'perception of the world', which does not just accept facts but also asks how and why. For a blind person, this means 'audible perception of the world'.

The basic function of our thinking device consists of the central processing of the five external senses, something which similarly applies to many animals. The forming of *terms* through deduction, or *abstraction*, of the essential characteristics of a primary sensual impression is applicable only to humans. This transformation of immediate impressions into terms works completely automatically in adults, while small children still live in a world of 'pictures'. Their first important building of terminology consists of the use of the word 'I', through which the whole world is separated into an 'I' and 'not-I' environment. The superficial linkage of terms is a matter of the intellect, which always appears as assistant to the I (Ego).

Belief in the encompassing abilities of the intellect is called rationalism. The nuclear physicist *F Capra* examines its cause and dangerous effects in his work, *Wendezeit (Turning Point)* (4). *Capra* does not only criticise this widespread attitude, but also points out more comprehensive ideas, which show humanity a way out of the current dead end. Logic (computer logic, mathematics) works according to strict rules, while speculation uses a lot of imagination.

Visible light serves as a good analogy to intellect, since it mainly shows us the surface of things. The longer heat beams, on the other hand, penetrate the substance deeper, and the much shorter X-rays even penetrate bones and metals.

MIND AND UNDERSTANDING *ANALOGOUS TO* ULTRAVIOLET LIGHT

In contrast to scientifically-oriented psychology, which owes its illumination to observations and experiments, one does not hesitate on the next level to penetrate the *supernatural* area, which is the task of *parapsychology*. It considers personality to be more than the person living on earth. According to the definition:

Personality = self-assured part of our soul that is *independent* from the terrestrial body

Figure 37

a human being is just as much a personality on an astral level, where s/he stayed *before* embodiment and where s/he will return *after* his/her departure from this earth. The only difference is that humans put on a rougher *terrestrial* dress in *addition* to their astral bodies. The astral body serves as the basis for the psychic emotions as well as for the physical sensations, which disappear during anaesthesia due to the separation of the astral from the worldly body.

In that connection, one often talks of the *higher vibrations* on more refined levels, which remain hidden from our primitive senses. Accordingly, ultraviolet light has a shorter wavelength and a *higher energy* than visible light, which is the reason why it can easily cause sunburn on light skin. The ultraviolet radiation in the stratosphere allows for the production of *ozone* (O_3) from common atmospheric oxygen (O_2). The ozone layer functions as an essential ultraviolet-filter for all living creatures, the assumed deterioration of which caused by the gas in spray cans has brought forth violent discussions. The healthy human *mind* will never run into walls the way experts and specialists keep doing. The term 'understanding' indicates interhuman qualities that make *tolerance* possible. 'I understand' is mainly a matter of the *heart*, while comprehension is limited to the *brain* (intellect).

COMMON SENSE, INTUITION AND ILLUMINATION *ANALOGOUS TO* X-RAYS

When the electromagnetic rays become even shorter, we reach the X-rays. Because of their ability to penetrate solid matter, they have become part of medicine and material testing. They are so full of energy that, without precautionary measures, the whole organism will suffer.

In our search for analogies for X-rays, we consider the fact that the shorter the wavelength of the light becomes, the more its frequency increases, i.e., its *power to penetrate*. X-rays linger less on the surface than visible light. The corresponding *psychic* area is found 'deep down', while the intellect depicts the *skin* of the human mind.

It has been emphasised that the personality, as a psychic complex or effect, exists on earth as well as on the astral level. On both levels of being, there is a duality between the Ego and the environment. All beings depend on other *similar* beings with whom they can *socialise*, either peacefully or aggressively. During this exchange, the sensual tools serve as mediators, even if the perceptions are supernatural.

Psychoanalysis offers us an area of psychic activity that is hidden under the surface of all personal life. C G Jung calls it the *Self*, and assigns the 'collective subconsciousness' to it, which has already been illuminated with the aid of the analogy of the iceberg (Figure 34). The Self is *independent* of everything personal and therefore able to create a multitude of persons, of whom only one usually becomes conscious in a terrestrial body. In that sense, we can consider the Self to be a chain that connects the embodied persons.

We are looking for a mental analogy for the penetrating power of X-rays, which let a physician see through our body as if it were made of glass. Similarly, the creatures that are freed from the duality of the astral world are described as being *transparent* in the *mental* world, which is the reason why they no longer have a shadow. On a psychological level, this corresponds to personalities who have overcome their constricting and darkening egoism. Furthermore, the saints are described as *shining, analogous to suns*, as can be read in *Dante*'s *Divine Comedy*. Since this illuminating power – invisible to worldly eyes – concentrates on the head, we find it depicted as a halo in many cultures.

According to *Kant*, we want to call 'the whole *upper* cognitive faculty' *common sense*. It differs from the superficial intellect, since 'superficial' in the psychic-mental sense is *analogous to* rough and low. The *intuition* that stands next to common sense in the title points to our irrational mental powers, which can be found in the subconscious (dreams) and superconsciousness, while the *ratio*, similar to the intellect, belongs to day-consciousness – therefore rationalism. Spiritual indications concerning *illumination* have already been given.

DELIVERANCE AND AWAKENING *ANALOGOUS TO* GAMMA AND COSMIC RAYS

X-rays, as well as longer waves including infrared, stem from the electron sheath of atoms. The atomic core, on the other hand, offers high-energy gamma radiation, be it during the natural disintegration of radioactive substances or during the artificial separation of a uranium atom. It is yet surpassed by cosmic radiation, which even penetrates deeply into the soil, and whose origin is unknown. Its quantum energy can stem from annihilation radiation processes, which *E Sänger* (21) suggested for powering his photon rocket at the beginning of the 1960s. Annihilation radiation physically means the dissolution of matter (substance) without any residue into radiation energy, while in modern nuclear power plants only one thousandth of the core material is changed into heat energy.

Perhaps you assume that the annihilation of radiation of substance into 'nothing' is *analogous to* the dissolution of our psychic-mental basis of being. What are the primary instincts of life? According to the major religious faiths, they are the *coveting* of things and the desire for certain experiences, in short the *hunger for life*, or thirst for existence. While the goal of most mystics consists of illumination and unification with God – unio mystica – great individual mystics such as *Meister Eckhart* have made the heretic (in a theological sense) demand: 'Go beyond God!' This equals *Buddha*'s request to dissolve even the most refined desire for a godlike existence and to definitely wake up – ('*Buddha*' means 'the awakened').

Four Levels of Tendencies *analogous to* Additional Forms of Energy

SURVEY

In Figure 8, a first survey of the great multitude of tendencies as 'principles of creation' was given by assigning the most important tendencies to the four *realms of nature*. Such a division may be useful from a scientific point of view; *esoterically*, however, it does not satisfy at all. Therefore, the author has divided all possible tendencies into four major groups that apply more to the *levels of being* than to the earthly realms.

According to Figure 51, the terrestrial (including the ethereal) world is on the lowest level. The nearest other world is called *astral level*, where most of the 60 billion souls linger. In India, it is called the World of Desire, since the *astral inhabitants* live out their nature of desires, and miss suitable companionship even more than on earth. The world of *pure forms* is open to those people who have learned to apply their thinking apparatus free of wishes and desires. Only a few of the mystics of all faiths achieve *formless* levels of being – surpassing the areas of highest godliness.

Levels of Main Tendencies and Terrestrial Forms of Energy

World, Level of Being		Level of Main Tendencies	Psychological Level	Earthly Energy Form
formless (pure consciousness)		mystic	individuality	wave energy
Fashioned, pure forms (radiating ideas)		mental	self, superego	energy of location, speed
astral (image-like)	worlds of desire	social	personality	chemical and heat energy
Terrestrial-ethereal		material	person, ego	energy of internal tension

Figure 51

On the one hand, the four main levels are layers like solid, liquid and gaseous substances on earth; on the other hand, they penetrate each other like radio waves in space. Furthermore, these levels or worlds are strictly divided in the same way that earthly landscapes differ in climate and vegetation. *Dante* bases his *Divine Comedy* on the famous trinity of hell, purgatory and heaven, each of which he subdivides into levels of joy and sorrow. *Dante* describes the corresponding tendencies in *analogous* external conditions.

Due to the fact that modern man, especially in the industrial countries, is much more worldly oriented than earlier generations, *material* tendencies have developed very strongly. On the one hand, they are aimed at one's own body, which is the only possession of billions of the poorest of the poor. On the other hand, the population explosion and the simultaneous growth of cities has led to a housing boom, which includes huts made of metal sheet as well as skyscrapers. This development creates a net of necessities, under which environmental protection and an ecological conscience gain ground much too slowly to be able to stop the destruction of our home planet. We often overlook the *embodiment* of our soul, without which we could not have stepped into our worldly existence, as the most important aspect of material tendencies.

While the (rough) material tendencies concentrate on the worldly level, the *social* tendencies, with their extremes of love and hate, have their focal point on the astral level. The astral beings are equipped with similar senses as terrestrial beings for contact with their refined environment, and *E Swedenborg* emphasised the similarity of certain astral areas to our earthly environment. Because of these similarities, *Buddha* usually summarised both areas as the *kama-loka* (world of desire), whereby desire consists of more than merely the worldly and paraworldly demands of our five senses.

The *mental* tendencies of modern man can only be assigned to the fashioned world – usually called mental level in Europe – with reservation. The light world has little to do with our mentality, or world of thinking, since our thoughts are usually projections or, according to *Plato*'s cave simile, *shadows* from a higher world.

It is generally acknowledged that only the smallest part of our mental abilities is developed. However, the attempts to awaken our latent talents explore the width more than the depth or height. This may be clarified with the help of the following comparison to sun and moon:

SUN	intensive source of radiation	*analogous to*	Self, transcendental consciousness	platonic ideas, radiating structures and beings
MOON	weak reflection of sunlight		Ego-thought, day-consciousness	reflection of sensual impressions, intellect, repetition

Figure 52

The *sun* is an old symbol of *godliness*, since all earthly life depends on its mighty radiation power. The *moon*, on the other hand, *reflects* only a small fraction of the sunlight that hits it, which is why we perceive the moon as being cold. Our intellect – as the showcase of our mind – reflects the sensual impressions *analogously*, since 'to reflect something' also means 'to think about something'. The intellect, in particular, creates the Ego-thought (I am I) among small children and keeps it up through all changes in life until worldly death.

Exaggerated egoism – emphasis on the I – is generally rejected as being damaging to the individual as well as to society. But the more subtle forms of egocentric behaviour remain hidden even to sociologists and psychologists – apart from the few who have climbed higher levels of meditation.

Our intellect is embedded in the day-consciousness, while the transcendental consciousness goes beyond space and time, the I and the environment. According to Figure 51, it corresponds to the Self or superego. The famous analogy formula of the fabulous *Hermes Trismegistos*, which is often summarised as follows, refers to these two levels:

> As on the bottom, so on the top;
> as on the top, so on the bottom.

or, in our description, simply:

the top | analogous to | the bottom

Figure 53

In the Middle Ages, these two levels used to be symbolised by the sun and the moon, of which Figure 52 lists only a few analogies. On the lowest rough level, we have the mass of worldly people who are being twirled around through innumerable rebirths in a sorrowful circle of existence. On the upper level, called mental world, or *rupa-loka* – world of (radiating) forms – in India, the pure light creatures are found, whose *internal happiness* radiates from the inside for an eternity. Here, there are no shadows, something that is still common in the central and bottom astral regions. Creative inhabitants of the earth raise their intuition and inspiration, like antennae, up into the intermediate realms, as high as the mental level.

In the following sections, we concentrate on energy forms corresponding to tendencies, with which radiation energy (Section 3, Chapter IV) is supplemented.

MATERIAL TENDENCY LAYER *ANALOGOUS TO* INTERIOR TENSION OF SUBSTANCE

The interior tension of a *solid* object is torsion and flexion, traction and pressure. The compressive and tensile stress of a bent mast, for instance, is always combined on opposite sides of the object. A bowman changes the pull force of his taut string into the kinetic energy of the shot arrow. While the thin spiral springs of a mechanical clock are stressed by inflection, energy is stored in the form of torsion within the thicker spiral springs of a garage door.

With *gases*, the internal tension expresses itself in overpressure and low pressure (vacuum). In many areas, such as noisy air drilling hammers, compressed air plays a role in energy transmission and storage. There is even energy within a vacuum, which is made use of in milking machines. Even though *water* can be compressed much less than air, it contains energy in relation to overpressure; this energy is utilised to run turbines.

The development of mechanical terms of energy is based on the physical experience of power, as we know from flexing our *muscles*. Furthermore, we can produce compressed air, something glass-blowers and musicians depend on. On the other hand, a baby does not have to learn how to suck its mother's breast. Constructors have often followed nature's example.

The title analogy suggests certain similarities on both levels. So material tendencies express themselves in the desire for certain things and resistance to unpleasant conditions, which somehow corresponds to tensile and compressive stress in a matter.

SOCIAL TENDENCY LAYER *ANALOGOUS TO* CHEMICAL AND HEAT ENERGY

We have already discussed in detail the heat energy created in atmospheric oxygen through *burning* wood and coal. All chemical reactions, however, come with a certain degree of heat. Many reactions can be converted whereby, according to the law of energy conservation, at least the amount of heat energy produced earlier must be used again. Therefore, plants require energy in the form of sunbeams (photosynthesis) for the production of sugar, starch and wood (carbohydrates) from the products of combustion – carbon dioxide and water.

This works accordingly for alterations in the state of *aggregation*. During evaporation and vaporisation of water, relatively large amounts of heat are bound, which become free again during condensation and formation of snow and ice. For this reason, the air masses seeping from the south over the Alps of middle Europe in warm windy weather heat up considerably, and the dry air offers an excellent clear view.

Since chemical energy is created by reactions between atoms and molecules, it serves well as an analogy to *social* tendencies. The basic powers in chemistry are attraction and repulsion, which we experience on a human level as the extremes of love and hate. An *efflorescent* body, where all molecules have their solid place but carry out irregular heat vibrations within their range, corresponds to a society ordered by laws, morals and habits. One talks of the degree of freedom here, something which also applies on a human level. A chaotic society in times of change, on the other hand, corresponds to a *gas* where each molecule can quickly collide with any other molecule.

MENTAL TENDENCY LAYER *ANALOGOUS TO* EXTERNAL ENERGY

External energy refers to the position and speed of a body. Most striking is *kinetic* energy, which grows with the *square* of speed. Since the speed on roads and tracks already smashes up a car completely during a collision, one can easily imagine the percussion force of a projectile with multiple sonic speed. In evaporating, meteorites entering the earth's atmosphere show the alteration of kinetic energy into heat energy, something which, in returning space missiles, can only be controlled through technical tricks.

The *potential* energy of water is used on a large scale, be it that a reservoir is located on a higher level or that artificial terraced gradients are built into a river. For the production of electrical energy by turbogenerators, the potential energy of water has to be first changed into kinetic energy before driving the turbine. Here, gradients of 4, 20, and 400 metres are equal to speeds of 9, 20, and 90 metres per second, which an object would also reach in a free fall from these heights. As an example of the constant change between potential and speed, you have the pendulum in motion, which could swing back and forth forever in a vacuum at zero-loss suspension, and which led to the analogy of Figure 15.

As the conservation of psychic and terrestrial energy has a central meaning to us, an astronomic example is mentioned here. Since coming closest to the sun in March 1986, *Halley*'s comet is moving away in a narrow elliptic orbit and is constantly slowed down by the attraction of the sun; thirty-eight years later, it will have only $1/70^{th}$ of its maximum speed, and will start on its return to the sun. This celestial body, therefore, acts *analogous to* a huge zero-loss pendulum.

Both forms of external energy are *relative*. Water only has energy for us in reference to a particular altitude. When we let ourselves drift in a river, we have the same speed as the water. We can only utilise the energy of its current on land, as used to be done by watermills. This relativity of external energy matches the *intellectual* tendencies, since these, contrary to higher qualities of thinking, are *related* to our *Ego*. However, as we have seen, the Ego does not form a still pool on which one could rely, but is rather like a blade of straw to which the human soul thrown into existence clings in order not to drown.

MYSTIC TENDENCY LAYER *ANALOGOUS TO* WAVE ENERGY

While the wave characteristics of light can only be detected through artifices, we can feel acoustic transmission of low sounds as vibrations. We experience the characteristics of *wave energy* more clearly on the water. The delusive impression that the whole body of water moves at the speed of the waves is disproved by a swimming seagull. The waves run beneath the bird and rock the seagull up and down according to the height of the waves.

The fact that water waves also carry energy with them is proven by *surf*, the utilisation of which is a rich field for inventors. *Where* does that wave energy come from? Usually from the wind, which may have produced it in storm centres far away. Waves can travel thousands of miles almost unnoticed as a long, flat *swell*. On a calm day, a tourist may wonder about the regular low waves that, when moving towards the beach, pile up to a high surf.

The energy forms listed in Figure 51 grow from bottom to top, if the potential and speed energy is extended to space missiles, comets and planets on the one hand, and includes gamma radiation in wave energy on the other hand. This hierarchy corresponds to the hierarchy of the levels of existence with their inhabitants and the four main tendency layers, topped by the mystic tendencies.

Since a mystic goes beyond our world of space and time (transcends it) and temporarily leaves his Ego-confinement, his environment disappears with his six senses (including the sense of thinking). Nothing personal remains in his superconsciousness of unspeakable bliss, even though his individuality develops more purely than that of the inhabitants of earth. The mystic tendencies behind it more and more exceed his low (material, social, mental) tendencies. For a great mystic, such as *Meister Eckhart* and others, these low tendencies dissolve completely even during his life on earth. He lives day and night united with divinity, no matter what his social status may be.

Chapter V
EMBODIMENT AND RE-EMBODIMENT

Embodiment of our Soul *analogous to* the Building of a House

SURVEY

Even though it is difficult to find similarities between a house and the human body, person and house are strictly *analogous*. The author published the complete analogy in the first comprehensive use of analogy rules in 1972 (6). Of these results, the *creation* of both structures – terrestrial body and house – is of interest to us, since knowledge of the steps for erection of a house gives us a deeper insight into the relation between body and soul. Here we follow the example of the initiated in order to deduce from the obvious earthly matters the seemingly inaccessible psychic-mental qualities and laws of higher worlds.

Modern man has let himself be seduced by the astonishing results of biological research into believing that all human mysteries are basically solved by this – at least with regard to his earthly existence. But even today, *essential questions* remain unanswered:

1. Let us think of so-called *accidental siblings*: the rather common and great differences between siblings, not only of a physical nature, but even more of a psychic-mental nature.
2. How can the fates of identical *twins* (12), who have physically identical blueprints, differ as much as those of strangers? Even though there are usually great similarities and many parallels to be found in the lives of identical twins, just one exception is

enough to cancel out the materialistic theory of the purely earthly conditionality of human beings (including biological heredity and environment).
3. Why is the *artificial insemination* of humans, who are supposedly nothing but 'naked apes', met with much less success than that of animals? The ratio of successful artificial insemination among human couples amounts to ten per cent. The artificial insemination commonly done to cows, on the other hand, has a success rate of over sixty per cent.
4. Who or what *controls* the combination of parental genes *during procreation* – a process with infinite possibilities of combination? Does the ready answer – 'coincidence' – satisfy the reader?

THREE BASIC FACTORS

As opposed to some materialists of his time, *Buddha* emphasised that *three factors* are required for the procreation of a child: the mother during her time of the month, the father, and the *mental seed*. This seed describes the *child's soul* pushing into being, with all the inherent tendencies that the soul carries with it from previous embodiments. We place it opposite the three factors for building a house:

Embodiment/Procreation		House under Construction
embodying soul		builder/owner
father	*analogous to*	architect
mother		construction company

Figure 54

The *builder/owner* is a person or institution that plans to erect a certain building. The *architect* develops a general project according to the builder's ideas, and then the detailed blueprints; he negotiates with the authorities and obtains favourable bids from the *building industry*.

Let us contemplate the three analogies individually. The *construction company* that will erect the raw construction delivers most of the material to the construction site; this corresponds to the expectant mother. The *pregnant woman* has to feed the embryo all its nutrition (including oxygen) via the umbilical cord. The biological contribution of the *father* appears to be a small task in comparison, since he only contributes the sperm for the fertilisation of the female ovum. The father, however, has to contribute essentially towards the support of mother and child. With regard to the building of a house, this task equals that of the *architect*, who is responsible for ensuring that all the work is carried out properly and in time. Because the blueprints stem from him, the architect has great responsibility in making sure that the house functions well and that the *builder/owner* will be happy with it for decades to come. Without the latter's energy, perseverance and buying power, nothing could have been started in the first place. This corresponds to the thirst for being of the *soul* – its drive to be embodied, which finally overcomes all worldly barricades.

ANALOGIES TO PROCREATION

Even before the parents consider having a child, the soul in question is filled with a *longing for life on earth* and is willing to take on the difficulties and tests that come with it, even though embodiment is experienced by the soul as something similar to imprisonment. The soul is still conscious of the main stations of the *earthly fate* waiting for it, while it lingers in the other world. However, during descent of the soul into thicker levels, its consciousness darkens and, in the intermediate realm, it adapts more and more to the limiting terrestrial rules.

What is the reason when *healthy* spouses who have regular sexual intercourse *cannot have a child*? Medicine has no answer to this question, as it does not know or want to acknowledge the soul as the third factor. According to Figure 54, this question can be answered easily: these spouses remain infertile because no infant's soul comes to them. This karmic obstacle is so frequent that there are too few children for adoption in wealthy countries. Therefore, white couples keep adopting more and more babies from poor countries.

In comparison with the *building of a house*, infertile couples can be compared to negotiations between architect and construction company, without a builder/owner who is interested in their offer. The abundance of children in poor countries shows that, in the other world (astral level), many souls are ready for a materially less secure life on earth in order to pay off their psychic-mental debts.

A harmonious or disharmonious relationship with parents and siblings may be part of the child's karma, since love and hate outlasts death (11). It is important for parents to familiarise themselves early with the *individuality* of the child's soul, which should not be forced into any kind of scheme of how to raise the child. Each child has the right to freely develop within the boundaries of family and culture. Often enough, however, children are physically or psychic-mentally *enslaved* and abused.

The previous question as to who or what controls the *selection* of the *genes* between mother and father can now be easily answered from an esoteric point of view: the *soul selects* from the biological material of both parents whatever most *suits its tendency* household and karmic inheritance. This should not make you wonder, because according to Figure 54, the embodying soul equals the architect, who tries to realise his notions and ideas of a new house within the limits of his possibilities. We can differentiate between three steps here:

Embodying Soul		Owner/Builder
tendency household / instinctive structure		notions of planned house
selection of suitable parents	*analogous to*	selection of architect and construction company
combination of parental genes		individual design of blueprints

Figure 55

The following formula shows how the biological conditions of procreation equal the various preparations for house construction:

Biological Conditions for Procreation		Preparations for Construction
female organism ready to conceive		building lot
uterus	*analogous to*	location for house
fusion of ovum and sperm		first drafts by architect

combination of parental genes		contract architect – owner/builder
descent of fertilised ovum	*analogous to*	order to construction company
settling of ovum in uterus		start of construction (laying of first stone)

Figure 56

If a large *building lot* equals the *female organism*, then we can assign the *location* of the planned house to the *uterus*. The third step is the *union* of the mother's ovum with the father's sperm, be it naturally or through artificial insemination. Figure 56 shows corresponding first *drafts* that are discussed between the owner/builder and the architect. Usually, these non-binding negotiations lead to a *contract* between the builder and the architect, listing the latter's duties and rights.

According to our analogy table, the *descent* of the fertilised ovum into the *uterus* equals the *order* issued to the *construction company*. The reader should take note of the simile of said *descent* to the condensation of the soul, which descends from a finer and accordingly higher level to the roughest of all levels. Therefore, the delivery takes place at the future birth, at which point the dressing and darkening of the soul is completed. With the combination of parental genes, the infant soul has its new *information carrier*, which can settle in the uterus and start *growing*. This equals the *start of construction*, usually celebrated with the laying of the first stone.

ANALOGIES TO PREGNANCY AND BIRTH

The *growth* of the seed, caused by cell division, involves approximately *forty doubling steps* from the fertilised ovum to birth. This is an enormous increase in size, since ten times a doubling already has the factor 1,000. On the other hand, the outline of the house is marked on a building lot prior to putting down the foundations. The house then only grows in height until it has reached its full size after the raw construction has been completed, even though it is not yet finished at all. The creation of our body is, therefore, totally *dissimilar* to that of a house, the same way as the finished person has hardly any similarities to a house. Yet person and house stand in *close analogy*.

Since the 1960s, science has shown an increasing interest in the embryo's *relationship* with its parents, in particular after the beginning of the sixth month. While one first concentrated on the physical and psychic influence of the mother, it is now known that the embryo also reacts to the father's behaviour. An essential factor is whether father and mother are looking forward to the birth, or want to stop it from happening. If the parents disagree, the disharmonious atmosphere between the spouses will disturb the development of the seed. Every change of mood of the mother is directly transmitted to the child that 'grows beneath her heart' – a term that should be understood literally and symbolically. According to the law of reciprocal effect, the child's soul also influences the mother, as the extraordinary moods and cravings of many pregnant women show.

What can be compared to these relationships with regard to *house construction*? The following can be deduced from the basic analogy of Figure 54:

the mother's affection for her growing child	*analogous to*	interest of the construction company in the new construction

Figure 57

In a harmonious relationship between the spouses, we expect:

marital love	*analogous to*	harmonious cooperation between building company and architect

Figure 58

The frequent question with regard to the continuation of *marital love* during pregnancy can also be answered by means of an analogy. Insofar as sex is an expression of love (a psychic-mental tendency), it is part of marital love according to Figure 58. Depending on the psychological constellation within the family, sexual intercourse is tolerated, or even desired, by mother and child (the embryo's soul) until late pregnancy. However, if sex only means physical craving without love, it more than likely puts a strain on mother and child. This would correspond to the opposite of Figure 58 – a disharmonious relationship between the three basic factors in Figure 54 and unfavourable preconditions for the child's birth and subsequent future.

Generally, the following analogy applies:

prenatal attitude influences the child's whole future life	analogous to	careful construction influences the owner's future quality of living

Figure 59

This connection does not only apply to a planned prenatal attitude, in the sense of parental responsibility, but also to the coincidental and frequently negative psychological-social conditions during pregnancy.

According to our previous analogies, the *descent* of the soul from the other world to its terrestrial embodiment equals the owner/builder's move. The following steps can be identified:

Descent of Soul		Owner/Builder's Move
stay of soul in other world (invisible from earth)		old place of residence (yet unknown at new place of residence)
visit of soul to mother	analogous to	visit to building lot
physical birth		move into house
weight of newborn		size of house

Figure 60

The soul that, until now, has stayed with its ethereal and astral body in the other world, is invisible from the earth. However, there are *clairvoyant individuals* who can *sense the soul* during its *visit* to the expectant mother. The frequency of such visits differs from case to case, just as the builder will appear more or less often on the building site according to opportunity and interest. If the house under construction is located very far away from his old residence, he has to mainly rely on his architect. According to Figure 51, this rare case corresponds to a soul that comes from a higher, finer sphere down to earth.

In the second to last line of Figure 60, three easily comprehensible items can be differentiated:

Physical Birth		Move into House
birth desired by family		on good terms with the neighbours
normal pregnancy (nine months)	*analogous to*	move into *finished* house
premature birth		premature move into house

Figure 61

There can be a variety of difficult circumstances accompanying a birth, such as an illegitimate birth that, in former times, could mean a horrible fate for mother and child, while it is only of minor importance in modern society. A builder who has built himself a house with limited means can, on the other hand, list a number of problems and disappointments – apart from considerably higher costs than his financial limit allows. It is now up to your own imagination to find the numerous appropriate similes!

Circulation of our Soul *analogous to* Year and Day

SIMILARITIES BETWEEN YEAR AND DAY

As a resident within the central degrees of latitude, you are familiar with certain similarities occurring between the course of the year and that of the day. The contrast between the day (half) and the night is reflected in the relation between summer and winter. Up north, where the midnight sun brings forth very light summer nights, which are similar to the day half, this becomes especially apparent. Vice versa, the sun does not rise at all for some period during the winter, which is why it is called an extremely long night.

The flora strictly follows the four seasons:

summer		growth, propagation
winter	*analogous to*	rest, recovery

Figure 62

This equals the daily rhythm of animals and humans (with some exceptions):

| day | | activity, growth, alertness |
| night | analogous to | passivity, rest, sleep |

Figure 63

Annual Course Similar to Day Course

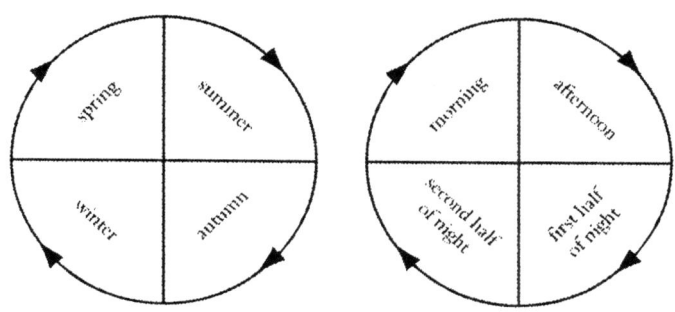

Figure 64

The periodical courses of year and day suggest coordination of their individual sections with each other, whereby we utilise the usual division by four. The similarity of time *sections* can be coordinated as follows:

Year		Day
spring		morning
summer	analogous to	afternoon
autumn		first half of night
winter		second half of night

Figure 65

While the length of the four seasons differs only little astronomically, the shifting of night and day, which are considerable in the polar regions and disappear at the equator, have already been mentioned. In this way, symmetrical circular division in Figure 64 is a simplified diagram.

When do these sections *begin*, according to Figure 65? They can easily be deducted from Figure 66:

Year		Day
beginning of spring		sunrise
beginning of summer	*analogous to*	noon
beginning of autumn		sundown
beginning of winter		midnight

Figure 66

The four sections of Figure 66 depict a skeleton that meteorology can fill out with the typical course of weather elements. Due to the region in question, the central courses of year and day are more or less similar. You could *summarise* the more detailed formulas of Figures 65 and 66, of which the previous analogies are subgroups:

Year	*analogous to*	Day

Figure 67

It is easy for the civilised human being of today to picture our globe turning in space. He finds it logical that the day half *on his side* equals the *night half* on the other side of the globe, where countries and oceans are in the earth's shadow. When the sun *comes up* on our side, it must at the same time *go down* on the opposite side. When there is spring on the northern half of the globe, the inhabitants of the southern half experience autumn.

The opposing sections in Figure 64, therefore, form not only time segments that run *successively*, but they also run *simultaneously*, yet in *opposite regions of the earth*: a remarkable coupling of space and time! If you make the effort to separately write down the two pairs of day sections and the two pairs of annual seasons listed in Figure 65, the opposite character of all phenomena will imprint itself on your mind and will sharpen your sense for the *opposite side of the coin*.

PERIODICAL CHARACTER OF A HUMAN LIFE

We have seen that terrestrial death forms a short-term *transition*, comparable to an opening door – *short-term* in relation to psychic-mental changes. If we compare the rough earthly level with *one* room and the fine astral level with an *adjacent* room, between the two of which a person *analogous to* a soul passes back and forth, we get the following clear analogy:

		analogous to	
this world:	terrestrial birth	analogous to	entering room
	terrestrial death		leaving room
other world:	astral birth	analogous to	entering adjacent room
	astral death		leaving adjacent room

Figure 68

Since the *door* between the rooms has no space for lingering, a person passes through it quickly and closes it again soon thereafter; the same way the 'door' is usually closed between the terrestrial and the astral worlds – this world and the other world. But the number of clairvoyant and sensitive persons for whom the door to the other world easily opens is steadily growing. This is also the task of mediums.

Birth and death are the *opposite sides* of each other. They are two aspects of the same process, only seen from the opposite side, as in the entering and leaving of a room in Figure 68. This opposite side is depicted in the following table:

Relationship between Death and Birth

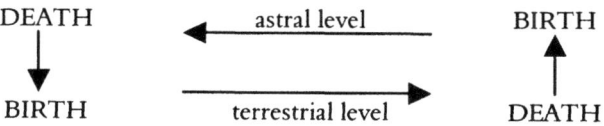

Figure 69

As death and birth are inseparably connected, we remember:

terrestrial death = astral birth
terrestrial birth = astral death

Figure 70

An illustration of this opposite side is the wave-like depiction of human life, according to Figure 71:

Wave-like Depiction of Human Life

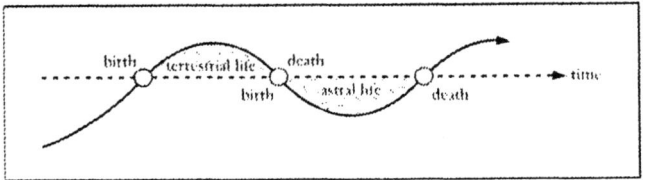

Figure 71

From our earthly point of view, the curved section above the time axis corresponds to our terrestrial life in flesh and blood. Below the time axis, we find the area of astral life that is concealed from terrestrial senses. When you extend the axis to the right with several terrestrial lives, you get an idea of the *continuity* of the human soul as a tendency formation in a series of embodiments, which *change* like an *actor's masks*.

CIRCULATION OF THE SOUL *ANALOGOUS TO* TIME PERIODS

Figure 71 corresponds to the Western attitude of unlimited progress, while the *circulating* character of all life is of greater importance in the East. However, in the mathematical sense, the wave-line in Figure 71 is *equal* to the circular movement depicted by arrows in Figure 69. In order to go more closely into the circular motion of human life, the two hatched sections in Figure 71 – above and below the time axis – shall be depicted separately as half circles in Figure 72:

The Two Half Circles of a Human Life

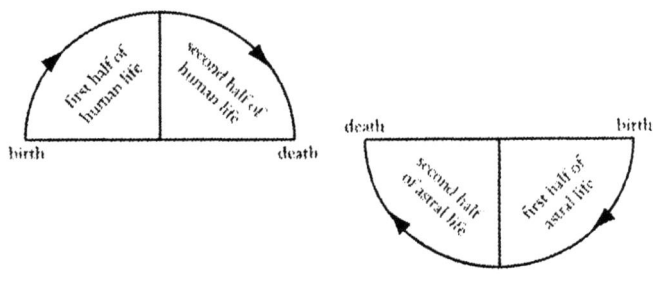

Figure 72

If we connect human life with the day half, the following analogies obviously apply:

Day Half		Terrestrial Life
sunrise		birth
morning		first half of human life
sun in zenith	*analogous to*	centre of life
afternoon		second half of human life
sundown		death

Figure 73

Some primitive races believe that the sun is born anew each morning, which can be explained with an analogy:

Phases of Sunrise		Phases of Birth
dawning (fading of stars)		pregnancy
aurora	*analogous to*	labour pains
appearance of sun on the horizon		birth itself
growing heat and light		baby's growth

Figure 74

Even though not all subgroups above can be reversed, there are also similarities between death and sundown:

Phases of Sundown		Phases of Death
diminishing heat and light		physical decay, diminishing worldly interests
disappearance of sun	*analogous to*	closing of worldly senses (death)
aurora		last tribute to deceased
Appearance of sun at other pole		opening of astral senses (resurrection)

Figure 75

At the point of death, the closing of *worldly* and opening of *astral senses* often occur *simultaneously*. This is obvious from the fact that the dying person recognises earlier deceased and tells his or her

83

terrestrial relatives about these apparitions. Usually, the souls are expected, and greeted from 'the other side', *analogous to* friends who, after a lengthy period of time, return from abroad to their worldly home.

While the terrestrial human is getting further and further away from his or her psychic side and focuses his or her desires on the terrestrial, rough, external world, the opposite happens with the deceased, apart from extremely materialistic persons. Like the earth, the astral world is experienced with *similar* physicalism, with all sensual organs as a continuum, and the terrestrial world slowly *fades* from the consciousness of the dying person like an *unreal* dream. So everything is relative! We are now able to supplement Figure 73 with the night half:

Night		Astral Life
sundown		terrestrial death
first half of night		first half of astral life
midnight	*analogous to*	climax of astral life
second half of night		second half of astral life
sunrise		terrestrial birth

Figure 76

We remember that terrestrial death = astral birth, and that terrestrial birth = astral death (Figure 70), since both are only different points of view of the same process.

The same way as principles of nature are simple and sometimes of breathtaking beauty, we may also trust the simplicity of the psychological and spiritual principles. We therefore combine the two half circles of Figure 72 – the day side and the night side of human life – into a whole circle. This circle is now *analogous to* a whole day, which we have depicted in Figure 64 as a circle. You can combine both into the following overall analogy:

day (24 hours)	*analogous to*	human life (terrestrial *and* astral life)

Figure 77

And, with the aid of the similarities found between the two periods:

year | *analogous to* | day

Figure 78

you can connect the last two formulas to a chain, in accordance with the first similarity and analogy rule:

year | *analogous to* | day | *analogous to* | human life

Figure 79

This *analogous* operation corresponds to the mathematical principle: if the values a = b and b = c are equal, a = b = c, i.e., a = c also applies. In our case, it follows from Figure 79 that the annual course corresponds to the course of a human life:

year | *analogous to* | human life

Figure 80

The knowledge of re-embodiment, or rebirth, is found among all primitive races. Two thousand years ago, it was also widespread in the Mediterranean region, as well as among Israelites and the first Christians. In the years 543 and 553, however, ambitious theologists in Constantinople condemned reincarnation as a false theory, and attempted to strike it from the Christian faith – something they succeeded in doing, apart from a few parts that were overlooked. The dogmas built up thereafter may be considered as the reason for today's lack of priests, and the fact that innumerable church members leave the church. Vital research by *H Bauer* (2), entitled *Reincarnation – You Were on Earth Before, You will Return*, is recommended to those who are interested in this part of church history.

Chapter VI
IMMORTALITY OF OUR SOUL AS A TENDENCY FORMATION

The Law of Mass and Energy Conservation

You learned in Section 2 of Chapter III that the 'Stability of Tendencies is *analogous to* the Inertia of Matter'. This qualitative relationship can also be proven quantitatively, since the principle of mass conservation applies to *classical physics*:

> The total mass of a closed system is stable.

Figure 81

This is logical since, through the *occlusion* of a particular system of masses, substance particles can neither escape nor can new particles enter. The whole art is to close a system one hundred per cent.

Our *planet earth*, which floats freely in practically empty space, comes very close to this condition. Apart from a constant stream of meteorites, we can theoretically consider the earth mass as being constant, without any geological catastrophes such as a glacial period, free nutations or floods being able to change this. The earth could expand or shrink, considerably extend its time of day, alter the chemical combination of the atmosphere, animals and plants could become extinct – and yet the total mass of the planet would still remain the same.

A *chemist* also applies the global rule (Figure 81) to the components of a reaction. As long as there are no nuclear reactions, the mass of each element stays the same before and after a reaction. This is expressed very well in reaction equations, where the sum of nitrogen atoms is about the same on both sides. Even through the most complicated transactions, not a single atom is lost in a 'closed system', nor are new atoms added.

Accordingly, no single tendency disappears in a *soul*, since no tendency can change without external influence. A *colourful sequence* in the conscious *appearance* of our tendencies can be observed, however, which makes a general survey of one's self-knowledge very difficult. Additionally, an external cause usually wakes *several* tendencies *simultaneously*, due to the fact that almost every object and every person is related to a *group* of *different* tendencies.

A rule *analogous to* Figure 81 applies to *energy*:

The total energy of a closed system is maintained.

Figure 82

However, in practice, it is much more difficult to close a system energetically than mechanically. The *globe* constantly *receives* sunbeams, part of which are absorbed, and on the other hand, it *radiates* heat day and night. Both processes depend on the type of surface, the density of clouds and the composition of the atmosphere – a global problem of *pollution*.

When we get *electrical energy* from a socket, the respective amount of water or heat energy, which may stem either from the combustion of coal or from nuclear fission, disappears from the power plant. On the other hand, you *change* the electrical energy at home in various ways: operation of a mixer, vibrations of speakers, heat for cooking and heating, light, and the operation of electronic devices. What happens to these energy forms in the end? They change into heat, which evaporates into the environment. And so the total energy of this extensive system is maintained.

Expansion Through Atomic Energy

While the two laws of traditional physics state that neither mass (substance) nor energy comes from nothing, or disappears without a trace, but rather they allow for *endless changes*, research into natural radioactivity cleared the way for an extension. Belief in the inseparability of atoms (atom means inseparable) had to be abandoned, and deeper and deeper insights were gained with regard to the interior of atoms. Science learned about the tiny, heavy *nuclear core*, where the characteristics of the elements are hidden, and saw the abyss of nuclear energy. Whether this happened to the advantage or disadvantage of mankind is yet unknown.

During the *natural* radioactive transition of extremely heavy elements, including uranium, while radiating alpha, beta and gamma rays, an astonishing discovery was made: in each of the three natural decay chains, the atoms are a bit heavier *before* the transition than *afterwards*, if the emitted mass elements are also considered. This *violated* the rule of mass conservation (Figure 81). Here, A *Einstein* found an elegant solution by putting the loss of mass Δm of a particular atom in relation to the released energy ΔE in the form of radiation and heating up:

Energy and Weight Assessment of an Atom according to A Einstein

	partial amounts		
$\Delta E = \Delta mc^2$		ΔE = energy gain	Δm = loss of mass
$E = mc^2$	total amounts	E = total energy c = light velocity	m = total mass

Figure 83

If you picture the total *mass* of an atom *decomposed* into many small steps – Δm = loss of mass; you get the corresponding energy amounts – ΔE – that add to the total *energy* – E – of said atom. Most famous is *Einstein*'s Formula, $E = mc^2$, for the calculation of total energy – E – from the atom mass – m –, with the help of light velocity – c.

Let us picture the *extent* of *atomic energy*! Even though only one per thousand of mass disappears during the fission of uranium in a nuclear power plant, and is gained in the form of heat energy, this amount is still fantastic enough. One gram of uranium mass (U-235) sets as much energy free as the combustion of 2,000 kilograms of heating oil. This is why atomic ships can go around the whole earth without 'refuelling'. In the nuclear power plant, nuclear energy is completely changed into heat to produce steam that – just like in conventional power plants – fuels turbogenerators for production of electrical energy.

When a uranium atom *bursts*, and completely new atoms are formed, the uranium atom is *dead*. An elderly human being dies not only from disease, but also because his/her *soul* has *tired* of terrestrial entanglements and *longs* for *liberation* from its physical confinement. During this separation from the body, a *mature* soul sets great psychic-mental powers *free*, which corresponds to the top lines of Figure 84:

longing of the soul for liberation from the earth (death)	*analogous to*	heat production through nuclear fission
longing of the soul for terrestrial birth		heat production through nuclear fusion

Figure 84

The peaceful use of atomic energy through nuclear fission coincides with an astonishing change in *human attitude* towards *death*. While rationalism and materialism had *suppressed* all issues dealing with death, we witness more and more public discussions concerning *dying*. The courageous and much honoured researcher into the issue of dying – Elisabeth Kübler-Ross – takes credit for a great part of this change of attitude.

Just as helplessly as the civilised person approaches the issue of death, he or she faces the issue of re-embodiment of the soul. The same way as *birth* is the opposite side of *death*, nuclear fission of heavy atoms is the opposite side of *nuclear fusion* of light atoms, which also set energy free. Our sun procures its energy requirement for its enormous radiation mainly from the fusion of four hydrogen atoms into one helium atom. More suitable for production of a helium atom through fusion are two atoms of the doubly '*heavy*' hydrogen (also called deuterium). There are as many as two deuterium atoms among 10,000 terrestrial hydrogen atoms. As they can be produced relatively easily, our oceans practically offer an inexhaustible supply of this 'fuel' for nuclear fusion. Unfortunately, in spite of intensive efforts, the nuclear physicists have not yet succeeded in gaining such a *stationary* process of fusion. Only *instationary* fusion was achieved by several states in the form of the horrible hydrogen *bomb*, using uranium bomb as the fuse.

Considering the bottom lines of Figure 84, you may ask yourself if powers of the soul are also set free in that situation.

This is correct, since the longing of the soul for the innumerable sensual impressions and possibilities of activity can be fulfilled through its embodiment. The satisfaction of that tendency group, which *Buddha* called the *thirst for being* according to the individual karma of the soul, evens out all problems and sufferings of terrestrial life.

Unlimited Ethereal Energy

The discovery and handling of atomic energy has esoteric aspects, since terrestrial substances – if only to a small extent – disappear and cannot be relocated anywhere. On the other hand, the radioactive radiation of different atomic cores indicates higher levels, since it cannot be influenced or even be stopped through any chemical or biological processes. The well known statement – that substance is frozen energy – can be expressed in greater detail as follows:

Substance (terrestrial material) is frozen ethereal energy, and therefore relatively stable.

In esoteric literature, however, one repeatedly comes across cases of dematerialisation and materialisation, as well as related appearances.

Since the revolutionary discoveries of physical science in 1904, many scientists, both here and abroad, have been trying to capture ethereal energy with suitable converters (new electrical devices) (26). The great Croatian physicist, *Nicola Tesla* (1856–1943), already had patents in this line of work. It is recorded that he converted a vehicle run by electricity, not with a battery, but rather with an antenna that drew electricity directly from the ether. Since this ethereal energy penetrates the whole universe, including the globe and our bodies, one may talk of unlimited and inexhaustible ethereal energy. The model of a 'closed system', as we saw in Section 1 of Chapter VI, is useless with regard to ethereal energy.

Why is it that discoveries with regard to utilisation of ethereal energy, also called 'free energy', have not yet had a breakthrough? Its fans claim that the industry boycotts its development, since users would become independent of public energy supply. The neglect of *psychological conditions* seems, to the author, to be the more important cause for previous failures. A few points shall be mentioned:

1. On the level of ethereal energy, the *reciprocal effect* between experimenter and observed object assumed by quantum physics applies generally between *all* objects and creatures, including human beings.
2. *Telepathy*, a subject which has already been mentioned earlier, is an indication of this fact. It works subconsciously even among materialists, but any human being open to it can observe its effects upon his or her environment.
3. It repeatedly occurred that an ethereal *converter*, which clearly produced net energy in the presence of its inventor/ constructor, *failed* in the presence of sceptical/critical visitors. Instead of talking about deception or fraud in these cases, one should remember that human beings automatically influence all areas of refined substance through their aura and thoughts – spiritual beings and a positive attitude work like a catalyst, while the opposite works like a blockade.
4. The first generation of *commercial* ethereal converters for the production of electrical energy that is 'free of charge' will, therefore, be *limited* to a small group of ethereally-spiritually developed personalities, for whom such converters perform with relative reliability – *analogous to* the first radio technicians whose reception depended on the skilled adjustment of their crystal 'detector'. The public electricity net will, therefore, be needed for steady supply of electricity to the population for some time.
5. Even though ethereal energy ('free' energy) is unlimited, a physical limit must be taken into consideration. The energy transformed from ethereal energy into electricity changes into heat energy in the end. Since this *waste heat* raises the temperature of the earth, future energy waste could have even worse effects than today's greenhouse effect caused by certain gases. This shows once again that mankind will only survive if a strong *responsibility* for all aspects of terrestrial life is developed.

Sphere of Influence of the Soul

In Section 3 of Chapter 1, we learned about the ethereal body as a mediating link. When the soul uses its terrestrial body as an instrument and *expresses* itself more or less well within it, this is only possible due to the *ethereal body* as *mediator* and *transformer*. The following table shows this function between soul and terrestrial body, i.e., between tendencies as the most refined forms and worldly energies as the roughest forms.

When we consider that *astral* beings are *free* from the terrestrial *need* to procure *food*, since an astral body consists of its own conditions, we do not have to wonder about a *life expectancy* 1,000 times more than that of a human being. Additionally, the upper (godly) astral levels, where every wish is fulfilled as in paradise, have another advantage: due to an internal and external harmony hard to find on earth, there is *no disease*.

The Esoteric Structure of Humans

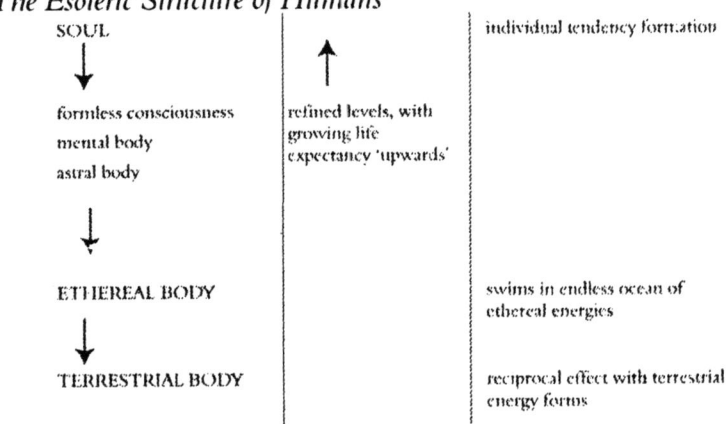

Figure 85

Of the group of three in Figure 85, the *mental* (fashioned world) gains a growing influence on modern humanity: *abstract* lines of thought can be understood as mental projections. The independence of the mental inhabitants by far exceeds that of the astral gods, since the latter are still very dependent on *contact* with their kind – the large group of social tendencies. The harmony-in-itself finds expression in the radiating physicality of mental beings.

Where everything radiates, the terrestrial change between *light and shadow* is missing, something that still controls the astral world, even if the intensity diminishes towards the top.

The astronomical *life expectancy* of radiating mental inhabitants, which surpasses that of astral inhabitants 1,000 times, is related to their *independence*. It is said of beings of *formless worlds* that they lack any physicality, and that they linger in a pure, intense consciousness of *heavenly peace*. Their life expectancy surpasses even that of mental beings to an unimaginable extent and is practically infinite, whereby we approach the timeless and immortal soul. *Buddha*, however, emphasised that even the highest of all mystic conditions of consciousness will enter rougher levels, *when* their latent *tendency levels*, which are aimed at lower worlds, according to Figure 51, will become active again.

The Rule of Tendency Changes

Before you can convince yourself of the 'immortality of the soul', you have to learn the rule of tendency changes. It would be a sad thing if we had to accept our tendency household the way it is. The point of view – 'this is the way I am, I cannot change' – seems to be too easy, and borders on fatalism. In fact, there are automatic tiny tendency changes that constantly take place *without* one being aware of them.

A psychological example of an *obvious* tendency change is a person who just *retired* after having eagerly worked in his profession, but who finds greater satisfaction in his *hobby* or passion. While others look back with longing to their lost position, this individual is happy to have *escaped* the rat race. On any occasion that reminds this person of his former profession, he will *dismiss* his former activity as 'no big deal'. Do you wonder if his interest in his former job is *fading* through such constant *negations* until it is more and more forgotten?

On the other hand, a person with a character weakness, such as sloppiness, sometimes succeeds in *developing* a stronger tendency towards neatness, i.e., love for neatness, through the habit of a *planned* regular *lifestyle*. The sexual drive can be sublimated the same way, *without* being suppressed. On the one hand, it is an animal instinct and biological programming; on the other hand, a psychic characteristic and *transworldly* energy. Usually, two tools have to be applied for such a fundamental change: the *negation* of blocking tendencies and the *affirmation* of supporting tendencies.

Psychoanalysis has contributed valuable work to our subject of 'tendencies', by proving that tendencies can be just as *effective* subconsciously as they are in a conscious state of mind. This is why the common suppression of social, emotional and mental difficulties is more an escape than a solution to the problems. *Reincarnation therapy* recently showed that occurrences and experiences from former – and not just from the most recent – terrestrial lives reach into the present.

There is a remarkable similarity between biological and karmic *inheritance*. Just as a biological characteristic, such as a special talent or an inherited illness, can remain *latent* through many generations, tendencies of the soul can remain passive during many incarnations, before they become active again under the right conditions in a terrestrial or higher life. Only *then* can they cross the threshold of consciousness.

The discovered characteristics of *tendencies*, those concealed and open internal energies, are summarised in the following *basic statements*:

1. Tendencies are transworldly *energies*.
2. Tendencies of constant intensity can remain *subconscious* for any length of time.
3. Tendencies can only become conscious during their *active* phase.
4. Only tendencies that have become *conscious* can *change* in their intensity and direction (quality).
5. *No* tendency change ever gets *lost*, but it can be annihilated again.
6. During the course of many incarnations, indefinitely *strong tendencies* and talents – all the way to genius – can come into being and then completely disappear again.
7. The stronger a tendency is, the *more often* and *longer* it becomes *conscious*, which improves the chance of changing it.
8. Tendencies *change* according to their positive and negative *evaluation*.

For a *planned* tendency change, you have to observe the basic rule, where you have to differentiate between three cases:

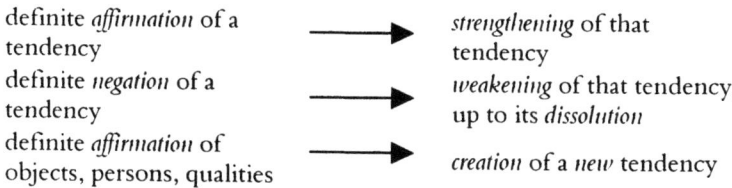

Figure 86

Since this psychological and spiritual principle of being has been mostly forgotten, the civilised individual faces his/her destiny/destination helplessly. One unwillingly admits his/her ignorance, with the popular explanation – *'coincidence'*. Figure 86, however, encourages the mentally striving person to take full *responsibility* for his/her *own life* and to courageously take destiny into his/her own hands.

The frequent *repetition* of a thought or an activity does not necessarily cause a strengthening of the tendency behind it. When the repeated process runs *automatically* and becomes a habit, it disappears, in many cases, from day-consciousness and becomes subconscious – which guarantees that the intensity and type of said tendency is maintained. However, if you *long* for an experience, such as enjoying a certain food, you strengthen this tendency, no matter whether you can satisfy it this time or not.

Buddha recommended the basic rule in Figure 86 to his followers and monks as a tool for their internal change, with the following clear words:

'Whatever you consider often, your mind leans towards.'

Here, *'consider'* does not mean an automatic line of thought that passes through our minds, but rather a planned internal *effort*. It may relate to the affirmation of a tendency already present (first line) or the creation of a completely new tendency (third line in Figure 86). In both cases, *inclination* is the same as tendency. For the weakening and dissolution of burdensome tendencies (second line), *Buddha* recommended imagining their *negative results* for oneself and others over and over again. *Buddha* mainly considered the heart, the soul, and the tendency household of a human being, not his/her birth, profession, or reputation.

Immortality of the Individual Soul

If you consider the following,

    soul   =   total of all active tendencies of a being

Figure 87

you can easily transfer the rules of tendencies as a unit to your soul. In Section 2 of Chapter III, we looked at the *static* aspect of tendencies in this analogy:

    stability of tendencies | *analogous to* | inertia of matter

This builds a *bridge* between psychological and physical energy.

On a physical level, no one believes any longer in a *'perpetuum mobile'*, i.e., a device that inexhaustibly supplies energy without a respective amount of energy disappearing elsewhere. We may, or even must, conclude *analogously* that no tendencies can be created out of nothing either, as would have to happen according to the *Christian dogma* of constant creation of new souls for the purpose of terrestrial embodiment.

The learning of new facts, especially when they contradict our 'engrained' image of the world, is a *great effort* and a *time-consuming* affair. Changing our likes and dislikes, habits, and tendencies is even harder. Surely, you observe this in yourself and others. In this case, however, during terrestrial death there is hardly any time left for a psychic-mental change.

If, on the other hand, dying comes *slowly*, the clarity and energy needed for a change are usually lacking. Death, therefore, offers hardly an opportunity for 'great deeds', even if there is the desire to make up for earlier mistakes. If nothing on the psychic-mental level changes through terrestrial death, then what happens to the enormous tendency energy of our souls? We have already learned about tendencies, according to Figure 3, which applies to each level of being:

    Tendencies =   psychic-mental *energies* that determine the
                         kind, direction and extent of all life processes

Figure 3

Your soul, as a transworldly energy complex, is *completely preserved* and, after losing its terrestrial dress and sensual tools, *searches* for a *refined substitution*, which is always available.

Analogous to the physical energy conservation rule (Figure 82), *no power* in the universe *can kill the soul*. In *suicide*, which occurs so often, only the terrestrial shell is destroyed. No one, however, would commit suicide if he or she knew of the horrible consequences. A person who has killed himself/herself will live through the internal and external preconditions of his/her deed over and over again in his/her astral body. A suicide is only saved at the point in time when s/he would have died a natural death on earth. The psychiatrist, Dr Carl Wickland, recorded tragic reports in *Thirty Years Among the Dead* (30/31).

As the existence of our soul is *not limited* by any rules, our soul is rightfully considered *immortal*. While a Westerner, hungry for life, may happily accept this certainty, many of *Buddha*'s contemporaries worriedly asked him: What do we have to do in order to *escape* this eternal circle of reincarnations? *Buddha* pointed out the way to *voluntary* dissolution of the soul – as a tendency formation (Figure 87) and transworldly energy complex, as the author understands it.

In order to comprehend the dissolution of the soul, which is only strived for as an exception, the rule of tendency changes (Figure 86) shall be coupled with *Einstein*'s equation, in accordance with Figure 83. In the section before last, we saw that, during radioactive decay of atoms, there is a loss of mass ($-\Delta m$) and that the corresponding amount of energy ($+\Delta E$) is radiated. Due to the close connection between tendency and substance (mass), according to Section 2 of Chapter III, the following analogy is applicable:

weakening of a tendency through negation (expansion of consciousness, liberation)	*analogous to*	$+\Delta E = -\Delta m\, c^2$ (radiation of energy, diminishment of mass)

Figure 88

By this psychological process of internal *detachment*, the dependence of the mentally striving person on his/her needs (tendency) is diminished. His/her freedom of choice, horizon and consciousness expand accordingly. From the Middle Ages all the way to modern times, this development of inner qualities was called the *'mystic path'*, something that is evidenced in all great cultures. The mystic's distancing and *turning away* from all kinds of worldliness gradually takes hold of the whole formation of tendencies and ends in *nirvana* = tendency-*free* condition. Almost all souls recoil from this 'nothingness'.

Due to the released energy, according to Figure 88, this nothingness, however, equals an expansion of consciousness into the unlimited, a view surpassing all times and space. *Nuclear physics* offers the following analogy on this issue:

complete dissolution of tendency formation (nirvana)	*analogous to*	disintegration of matter into radiation

Figure 89

The complete disintegration of matter into radiation occurs most elegantly through the corresponding 'antimatter': atoms of the same mass, but with opposite charge distribution. Antimatter forms an analogy to the 'tendency-eating tendency', i.e., the tendency that is aimed at dissolution of all other tendencies, and also disappears when the mystic enters nirvana. It was the genius E Sänger (21) who suggested that the disintegration of matter into radiation could be used to power his hypothetical photon rocket. He claimed that, with this method, as compared to all other powering methods, he would approach light velocity and could reach the next fixed stars within the time period of a human life.

The analogy opposing Figure 88:

strengthening of a tendency through affirmation (constriction of consciousness, bondage)	*analogous to*	$-\Delta E = +\Delta m\, c^2$ (binding of energy, increase in mass)

Figure 90

indicates the *magic path* the worldly human being uses by *identifying* more and more with terrestrial matter and the goods produced therefrom. He/she automatically becomes rougher and heavier, and sinks *downwards* on the ladder of being. Moral decay, economic chaos, nuclear armament, terrorism and destruction of the environment are mere side effects of this phenomenon.

Chapter VII
MEDITATION AS MYSTICAL SOLUTION FOR OUR SOUL

Introduction

If you have followed the author to this point, you have rediscovered your soul, that transworldly energy complex. Meditation will be a welcome means for you to utilise your internal treasures for your worldly *and* mental life. Let us see what the noted Catholic priest, *Klemens Tilmann*, as an experienced meditation supervisor, says in the introduction to his *Practice Book on Meditation* (28):

> An astonishing process is taking place in modern human beings: *they long for meditation*. Independent of their faith and view on life, they sense that in the stress, noise and haste of life they are about to lose their best and essential, that *deep down* they are becoming frustrated and feel empty inside. That is why they ask for something that leads them into their depth... (p. 9)
>
> Meditation is easy and, in a way, child's play – every undisturbed child meditates till about age ten. On the other hand, it requires a long way for all those who want to rediscover it and grow within it. (p. 17) *by H. De Witt*

Some of the most common misunderstandings with which a Westerner confronts 'meditation' shall be clarified first. For several centuries, 'to meditate' has supposedly been *thinking* about a philosophical-religious subject. On the one hand, 'correct thinking', the way *Buddha* meant it, is a necessary *tool* on the long road of meditation. On the other hand, we have to become able to *free* ourselves from our *urge* to think, the same way as you would turn off a record. The extroverted Westerner who usually *identifies* with his/her thoughts is, therefore, at the mercy of this *automatism*.

While the average Westerner easily *concentrates* on external things, s/he has great difficulty in applying this ability to processes occurring in his/her *internal* world. Even important meditation schools almost suggest that concentration is identical to meditation. However, no one will reach salvation through intense concentration, as the following analogy shows:

Internal Attitude		Type of Lighting
concentration		sharp beam of rays from spotlight
dispersion	*analogous to*	flickering candlelight
meditation, attentiveness		broad light from large lamp

Figure 91

Concentration focuses the attention as mental energy on a detail, and keeps everything else in the dark, while *dispersion* effects the opposite. The worldly human being sways between these two extremes. On the other hand, meditation means *alert* attention that is *aware* of all thoughts and feelings, wishes and impulses of the will, *without* excitement; identifies with *none* of them, but rather lets all *pass* unbiased. This is the core of the *attentiveness* or *mindfulness* with which even nirvana can be achieved.

Since even dispersion still means *tension*, we all need periodical *relaxation*, which can only partially be obtained through sleep. However, *physical* relaxation, such as during autogenic training, is not sufficient. For meditation, it has to be supplemented with *psychic-mental* relaxation. For the Faustian European, this is easier said than done, as s/he lives to work, while the more relaxed Easterner works to live.

How are *prayers* related to meditation? Prayer is usually aimed at a personal God and other transcendental beings, be it for the fulfilment of wishes or protection from danger. Prayer and meditation have in common that one turns to the *inside*, but their *goals* differ. We get an indication of this in the demand of great mystics such as *Meister Eckhart* and *Angelus Silesius*: Go beyond God! With this heretical sentence, they have transgressed the *dogmatic* limits of their church and entered the *infinite* area of meditation.

Mental Preconditions for Meditation

What is the 'mystic way out for the soul' from its sorrowful and insecure existence on earth? *Paul Brunton* answers this question in his book *The Way Inside*. Here, we must turn away from the external world that has brought us material abundance, but also high divorce and suicide rates, alcohol and drug abuse.

This *internal* solution must *not* be mixed up with an *escape* from the *external* world. No monastery guarantees us the inner liberation demanded by all mystics, which, on the other hand, will not release us from the *obligations* we have in this world. Quite a few individuals have misunderstood *askesis* and got themselves into new debt. The *golden centre* will always remain a new challenge to the true seeker of God.

The ancient demand for *self-knowledge* can be better fulfilled in the world than in seclusion, *if* our *environment* serves as a *mirror* of our own personality. More clearly than 'dead objects', the people around us, through *their* behaviour, let us discover what is happening *inside of us*. How often do we 'discover the splinter in our brother's eye, but overlook the beam in our own eye'. This saying describes our inclination towards *criticism*.

Even one who admits this weakness to himself/herself will dodge from the following psychological rule:

criticising others | *analogous to* | one's own faults and weakness

Figure 92

Everything that particularly *strikes* you in your surroundings, and which *evokes* critical thoughts in you, is proof of *corresponding* characteristics and faults in *yourself* – no matter whether your observations are correct or not. The *echo* from your subconscious is evidence enough, even if you do not express your critical thoughts. Isn't that a fantastic source of self-knowledge? And an almost inexhaustible one?

We reach *attentiveness or mindfulness* that, according to the third line of Figure 91, equals the broad light from a large lamp.

Attentiveness is a higher degree of *alertness*. If you ask an average person when s/he is especially alert, s/he will probably answer: when I do some serious thinking. This is the highest level of alertness, which *Homo sapiens* realises in *Descartes'* 'I think, therefore I am'. The whole of modern civilisation is caught in this *dead end*, which has to result in troubles on all lower levels.

As an alert, sharply conscious human being, you do not only have an advantage over your contemporaries in everyday life. You also hold the *key* to final liberation. Therefore, here are some indications of that rare and valuable talent, with which the inner realm of soul and mind will be unlocked after years of use on a regular basis. A central position in practical *Buddhist* meditation is *passive observation of breathing*, whereby breathing may *not* be influenced at all. The mysterious effect of this exercise has to do with the position of the diaphragm between the chest and stomach areas in the centre of the body.

As introductory texts to this meditation method, I can recommend:
1. By the German monastic scholar in Sri Lanka, *Nyanaponika*: *The Only Way, Buddhist Texts on Mental Training in Correct Alertness* (20).
2. By *Josef Goldstein* (USA), who harmoniously combines Eastern wisdom and meditation practice with the clarity of Western thinking and acting: *Vipassana–Meditation, the Development of a Clear Consciousness* (13).
3. By the German, *Ayya Khema*, who founded her first convent in Sri Lanka and is known as a meditation teacher all over the world: *Buddha without Secrets, His Teachings for Everyday Life* (16), which does not require any knowledge of Buddhism.

Conditions of Main Consciousness

Since meditating individuals strive for a higher consciousness, the most important conditions of consciousness shall be described. Our normal sleep is interrupted every night by *dreams*, which are necessary as a supplement to terrestrial life when awake, and correspond to astral consciousness. Daydreams may occur just as often, when our consciousness *slips* from the hard and sorrowful daily life into wishes, fantasies and memories. Rare *deep sleep* is not interrupted by dreams, and offers the highest degree of relaxation and recreation to body and mind.

Instead of the 'condition of being awake', we had better say *day-consciousness*, as this is tied to the terrestrial body. The flood of sensual impressions processed by our intellect and the image of the world built on that are similar to an iridescent soap bubble, at the centre of which an Ego is experienced. The *intellect* corresponds to the way to the *outside*, whether it is dedicated to astronomy, nuclear physics or medicine. This intellect has always been *confused* with the *mind*, as a third factor, and this is the cause of the misunderstanding that thinking is already meditation.

We owe considerable expansion of our image of the world to the increased interest in meditation since World War II. In 1970, *Robert Keith Wallace* suggested, in his dissertation, a *fourth* condition of main consciousness that *clearly differs* in the pattern of brainwaves and other physical functions from the types of consciousness with which we are already familiar. A group of TM-test subjects made statistically-recorded findings possible for the first time. In 1976, *H H Bloomfield* and others (3) summarised the most important research results in comparison to non-meditating individuals in a comprehensible report.

In the meantime, the meditation method developed by *Maharishi Mahesh Yogi* has spread all over the globe and Transcendental Meditation (TM) has wakened the interest of science and other experts. '*Transcendental*' means 'transgressing day-consciousness', and this higher condition of consciousness is therefore – opposite to subconsciousness – also called superconsciousness, to which the superego is assigned. You could also call it *background consciousness*, by imagining that there is a *still observer* in the background of your daily activities who checks everything – *without* ever intervening. You can consider him to be the representative of alertness. In the film analogy (Figure 48), the white screen represents the transcendental or background consciousness. Just like the still observer, the white *screen* will not be touched by the day's experiences in space and time, which are *analogous to* the film scenes projected on the screen.

Even though a growing tendency towards Eastern wisdom is observed in the Western world, there are still many prejudices against *Buddha*'s doctrine of salvation. Unfortunately, his unique and complete soul teachings have remained almost completely unknown. *Buddha* mainly considered himself a *curer* of the *souls* of his suffering contemporaries. As the final and deepest cause of all suffering, we have become familiar with our thirst for being, which has three roots: desire, spite and delusion. To work on the *diminishment* of these as defilement, poisons and chains of the soul is considered by all great religions as the awakening of *virtue*. Its development is part of the great preparatory period for meditation. Too often, humans try to evade this hard work and cheat their way to the sweet fruit of meditation through drugs, or by other means.

Based on his own experience, *Buddha* differentiates between eight higher conditions of consciousness, which are mostly translated by rapture or ecstasy. Already, the first rapture fills not only the mind, but also the terrestrial *body* of the meditating individual with such *bliss* that the mystics talk of 'the temple of God'. Figure 52 shows a simile on the relationship between transcendental and day-consciousness. Those who are interested in Buddhism as psychology are referred to the introduction to the complete teachings of Buddha by *Paul Debes* (10).

Chapter VIII
SUMMARY

The Soul as an Energy Complex

The basic question of human existence is: does the decomposition of my terrestrial body also mean the destruction of my conscious being? Dreams alone indicate that our souls can exist *independently* from our bodies.

Let's use driving a car as a simile/analogy for clarification of this fundamental question. In the following small analogy table, 'soul' stands for the completeness of the senses, thinking and desires (i.e. the *'mind'*):

| driver | | soul |
| car (automobile) | *analogous to* | (physical) body |

Figure 93

This analogy table can be interpreted as follows:

> The driver *controls* his car in the same way as the soul controls its body.
> In the same way that the driver can *stop* the car and *get out*, the soul leaves the body while *dreaming*.
> In the same way that a driver can move independently as a *pedestrian*, the soul enjoys an unspeakable *freedom* before and after its incarnation.
> In the same way that a car *parked* in a garage is a useless object, the *sleeping* body cannot be used for any worldly activities.
> In the same way that a driver can drive a *series of cars* over the years, the soul procures *new terrestrial bodies* over the centuries.

While the fourth section deals with reincarnation, the energy complex of the soul as a tendency formation shall be researched first.

The Soul as a Formation of Tendencies

So far, we have seen that the soul is the *enlivening* element in the body, which the author has defined as follows:

> Soul = completeness of all *active* tendencies of a living being

Tendencies are *focused* inner energies, which not only find their expression in the body, but can already become conscious earlier. In comparison, a beam of light, a jet of water, wind or a shot object have *focused* energy, but not the energy of warmth and pressure that aims in all directions.

In order to gain a first impression of the extremely versatile motivating energies of the soul, the following four groups are mentioned:
1. Condition of *inclination*: affection and dislike, sympathy and antipathy, love and hatred.
2. Suffering a *deficiency*: wish and need, longing and desire, drive and urge.
3. *Tension* between inside and outside: expectation and apprehension, hope and disappointment.
4. Conscious *pursuit*: drive and interest, ambition and striving for power.

It has been shown that it is useful to group all motivating psychic energies into tendencies:

> tendencies = psychic-mental *energies* that determine the kind, direction and extent of all life processes.

Figure 3

The above-mentioned *direction* of an energy is contained within the kind (quality) of life process in question.

You have to imagine that, over time, the tendencies of a soul have grown into a barely distinguishable *network*. Here lies the difficulty of psychotherapy, which in many cases can be solved by reincarnation therapy, by *going back* in *memory*, step by step beyond the patient's last birth.

The Embodiment of our Soul

Before we turn to re-embodiment, it is worthwhile examining the various conditions for embodiment. The opinion that the sciences of biology/medicine have answered all questions concerning procreation is still widespread. Let's consider healthy spouses whose wish for children is not fulfilled. In this case, artificial insemination only rarely meets with success, even though artificial insemination of cows shows a success rate of over sixty per cent. Here, biology obviously ignores the human mental aspect: i.e., that which separates human beings from the non-individualised animal.

Buddha emphasises that *three factors* are required for *procreation* and the conception of a child:

the *mother* during her period of conception;
the *father*;
the mental seed,

which circumscribes the *child's soul* that pushes into being. The child is, therefore, neither a biological copy of its parents nor an accidental creation of a god. It is rather an *ancient individual soul* joining the parents in order to accept another earthly embodiment. However, if no infant soul is ready to embody with a certain parental couple, the couple's desire and efforts remain fruitless.

The Re-Embodiment of our Soul

You experience a kind of re-embodiment on the smallest scale whenever you wake up in the morning and pick up your daily life where you left off the evening before. Even though many dreams are merely caused by physical functions, dream research proved that these periodical dream phases, when the soul leaves the body, are essential for our health.

Thanks to artificial light, we are less dependent on the course of the sun than previous generations. But have sunrise and sundown, therefore, lost their attraction? Hardly – but which tourist, taking a picture of the *sun disappearing* in the ocean, is conscious of the fact that, at that very moment, the *sun* is *rising* on the *other side* of the earth? This astronomical connection is part of the two sides that show a process from two opposite points of view – just like the two sides of a coin.

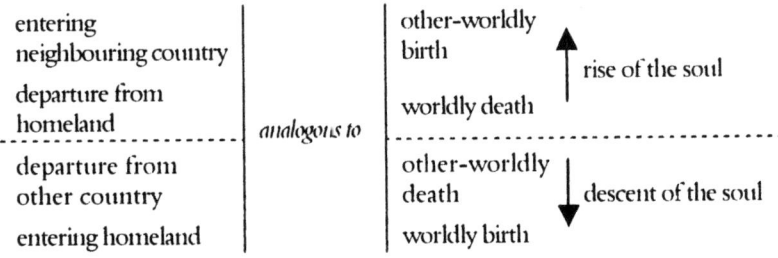

Figure 94

The other side of a border between two countries serves well as an analogy to the *mysterious connection* between *death and birth* in the above table.

This formula consists of two opposite sides: the top two lines describe the *rise of the soul*, after it has extricated itself from its worldly confinement (through 'death'); the bottom two lines describe the exact opposite process, whereby the terrestrial birth depicts only one side of the coin. With regard to a birth, we should always remember that any pregnancy is connected with the *descent of a soul* from a more refined world.

In this comprehensive meaning, birth and death only form the cross marks of the eternal wanderings of a soul through a rougher, worldly embodiment, and then again a more refined embodiment in other worlds: depicted by a *wavy line* (Figure 71) running through a straight line that symbolises the time axis. The length of the periods above or below that axis (worldly life, other-worldly life…) can differ immensely – based on the quality of the soul's tendency formation and the accomplished mental level.

The Immortality of our Soul

Based on the generally accepted physical law of the *conservation* of all *energies* – with multiple energy conversions – one can assume the conservation of the tendency energies of the soul, which are just as numerous. Since, for the author, the term 'soul' contains the total of all *active* tendencies of a being, the conservation of the tendency energies results in the immortality of the soul.

This theory is supported by the science of atom physics. The following analogy table shows the basic structure of an atom on the left, and the general tendency formation of the soul with its incarnations on the right – be it here on earth or in a higher sphere.

ATOM in Compositions		SOUL in Embodiments
tiny superheavy *nucleus*		tendency formation (pure energy *without* expansion)
light *shell* of electrons (less than one per cent of nucleus substance)	*analogous to*	chain of embodiments (Ego – environment, interest range)
interaction with other atomic shells (*chemical* compositions)		*social* relationships (society)

Figure 95

It is rightfully said that humans are social beings. In a society, a person's individual characteristics take second place in the interest of a variety of *relationships*, which suggests analogies to chemical compositions. In conformance with the bottom line of the analogy formula, the atomic shells interact with each other, i.e., a slight exchange of electrons takes place.

The shell of electrons enables the atom to expand, since the diameter of the nucleus is hardly 1/10,000 of the exterior diameter. In the same way as electrons cover the nucleus, each embodiment *dresses* up the *soul*. The naked soul as a tendency formation or as a transworldy energy complex is *invisible*, which is similarly true for the atomic nucleus. The only evidence of their existence is given by their traces. When disregarding the radioactive nucleus, you can say about both sides of the profound analogy:

Both are spaceless and ageless, i.e., immortal.

EPILOGUE

In this book, the author has only rarely pointed out if an analogy is tight/strong or loose/weak. In spite of the fact that *similarities* apparently have innumerable *grades*, ranging from extremely similar to rather dissimilar, this aspect has been rather *neglected* in analogies by *other* authors. For this reason, the analogy method lost its former meaning in comparison with the principle of *causality*, which has been gaining importance.

However, when you want to work with analogies – whether forming lengthy analogy *chains* or examining *subgroups* up to the higher order, you will be forced to carefully observe the *grades of analogy*. Otherwise, it will turn into a mere non-committal triviality. In order to circumvent this danger, the author has introduced special *symbols* for *three grades* of similarity, which also apply to the analogy relation, and for three grades of dissimilarity, in his three-volume standard book *Analogik* (6) and (8). With the aid of these symbols, you can create concise analogical formulas based on the *five laws* of analogy written down by *de Witt*.

BIBLIOGRAPHY

1. Bailey, Alice A: Esoteric Healing
2. Bauer, Hermann: Wiedergeburt–Du warst schon öfters auf dieser Erde, Du wirst wiederkommen. Universelles Leben, D-97070 Würzburg 1982
3. Bloomfield, Harold u a: Transzendentale Meditation, Lebenskraft aus neuen Quellen. Econ Verlag Düsseldorf und Wien 1976
4. Capra, Fritjof: Turning Point
5. Chatwin, B: Traumpfade. München, Wien 1990
6. de Witt, Hermann: Analogik Band 1 'Die Analogie zwischen Person und Haus'. Analogik Verlag 1989^2, CH-6045 Meggen/Luzern
7. de Witt, Hermann: Analogik Band 1, Analogik Verlag 1989, CH-6045 Meggen/Luzern
8. de Witt, Hermann: Analogik Band 2, Analogik Verlag 1982, CH-6045 Meggen/Luzern
9. de Witt, Hermann: Standardwerk Analogik Band 1, 2. Auflage Analogik Verlag 1989, CH-6045 Meggen/Luzern
10. Debes, Paul: Meisterung der Existenz nach der Lehre des Buddha. In 2 Bänden herausgegeben vom Buddhistischen Seminar, D-95463 Bindlach 1982
11. Desmond, Shaw: Die Liebe nach dem Tode, ein Blick in die Himmel und Höllen irdischer und himmlischer, Liebe. English edition: Love after Death. Hermann Bauer Verlag, Freiburg/Br. 1959

12. Friedrich, Walter: Zwillinge. VEB Deutscher Verlag der Wissenschaften 1983

13. Goldstein, Josef: Vipassana-Meditation, die Entfaltung der Bewusstseins-Klarheit. Frank Schickler Verlag, Berlin 1978. English edition: Vipassana-Meditation, the Development of a Clear Consciousness

14. Heyer, G R: Der Organismus der Seele. Kindler Verlag, München 1958

15. Hinz, Walter: Woher-Wohin. ABZ-Verlag, Zürich 1980

16. Khema, Ayya: Buddha ohne Geheimnis, die Lehre für den Alltag. Theseus Verlag, Zürich 1986. English edition: Buddha without Secrets, His Teachings for Everyday Life

17. Kübler-Ross, Elisabeth: Questions and Answers on Death and Dying.

18. Kübler-Ross, Elisabeth: Was können wir noch tun? Antworten auf Fragen nach Sterben und Tod. Kreuz Verlag, Stuttgart 1978

19. Norwood, Robin: Women Who Love Too Much: When You Keep Wishing and Hoping He'll Change. June 1986

20. Nyanaponika: Der einzige Weg–buddhistische Texte zur Geistes-schulung in rechter Achtsamkeit. Verlag Christiani, Konstanz 1970. English edition: The only way, Buddhist Texts on Mental Training in Correct Alertness

21. Sänger, Eugen: Raumfahrt–heute, morgen, übermorgen. Econ Verlag, Düsseldorf, Wien 1964

22. Schrödter, Willy: Heilmagnetismus, Quellen der Gesundheit. Aurum Verlag, Freiburg/Br. 1987

23. Sheldrake, R: Das Gedächtnis der Natur. Piper Verlag, München 1993

24. Sherman, H und Wilkins, Sir H: Sendestation Mensch, Telepathie auf dem Prüfstand. Ingse Verlag Zug 1974

25. Swedenborg, Emanuel: Die Wonnen der Weisheit über die eheliche Liebe. Swedenborg Verlag Zürich, Nachdruck von 1891

26. Tagungsband internationaler Kongress 'Freie Energie' Einsiedeln/Schweiz 1989. Zu beziehen durch SAFE, Postfach 402, CH-8840 Einsiedeln

27. There is an expanding literature on psychosomatics

28. Tilmann, Klemens: Übungsbuch zur Meditation–Stoffe, Anleitungen Weiterführungen. Benziger Verlag Zürich, Einsiedeln, Köln 1973

29. Wallimann, Silvia: Brücke ins Licht–ein Ratgeber für das Leben und das Leben danach. Verlag Hermann Bauer Freiburg/Br. 1986

30. Wickland, Dr med Carl: Dreissig Jahre unter den Toten. Otto Reichl Verlag, Darmstadt 1957. Additional title:

31. Wickland, Dr med Carl: Thirty Years among the Dead

32. Wilson, R A: Die neue Inquisition. Irrationaler Rationalismus und die Zitadelle der Wissenschaft. Verlag 2001 Frankfurt/M 1992